TANGLED

BROKEN: BOOK 2

TT KOVE

ARCTIC CIRCLE PRESS

PART I
CHAD

CHAPTER 1

The past two weeks have been awkward.

Living with two men: my former teacher, whom I was in love with, and his boyfriend, whom he cheated on with me, makes for a precarious situation.

They're both nice to me, but the awkwardness is still there. None of us know how to act around each other. Jeremy said he wouldn't mind the three of us trying out a relationship, but so far nothing has happened except awkward tiptoeing.

Only today I wasn't so much tiptoeing as running around a frantic, stressed mess.

"Calm down." Dion grabbed my shoulders and forced me down on the sofa. My knees kept jerking, I couldn't sit still. "You've taken your medicine today?"

"*Yes.*" I had been good the past two weeks, taking my prescribed dosage. "Today's special."

"You're going to work. Nothing special about that." His brown eyes were warm and caring, but his hands were firm on my shoulder, keeping me there on the sofa.

"Of course there is!" My anxiety was amping up by the second. "It's Harriet's dream. I have to do well. Not to mention my coworkers. I assaulted the boyfriend of one of them, and threatened the other with a knife. They must *hate* me."

"Of course they don't hate you." Dion finally let me go as he sat down beside me. "They know it wasn't you."

"But it was me." I laughed hysterically. "That was *me*. That's what I'm like when I'm not on medicine to stabilise me. That's me, uncensored." Now that I wasn't being held down, I jumped back up and started pacing.

Dion's gaze followed me. "Jeremy's there. He likes you."

"Does he?" I spread my arms wide, then tangled my fingers in my hair and tugged in frustration. "I can't do this. I can't. I'm just going to have to tell Harriet I can't come."

"Nonsense." Dion stood and came over to me, his arms wrapping around my shoulders in a hug. "This will be good for you. Getting out, doing some work. It's only for a few hours, until Jeremy's off. You'll come home together."

Hearing Jeremy would be there calmed me somehow. I knew he'd be there already. He'd been working there for a week now helping Harriet. At the moment he was doing both the Café and his old job. But hearing Dion say it calmed me down a bit. Even if things were the most awkward between Jeremy and I.

"Do you want me to walk with you down to Soho?"

I turned around as far as I could with his arms still wrapped around me and blinked up at him. "Why are you even home?"

He frowned slightly. "It's Saturday."

Oh, right. Days seemed to just fly by and into each other when I didn't have work or college to go to. I'd been at home for two weeks doing nothing, except heading out for doctor's appointments and psychiatry sessions.

"So would you like that? For me to head down with you?"

"Yeah." It came out on a sigh and I leaned against

him, the thought of starting a new job exhausting all of a sudden.

He massaged my scalp gently, cheek resting against the top of my head. "This is going to be okay. You'll be working with Harriet and Jeremy, and they'll both be there to look out for you."

I knew they wouldn't let me do something I wasn't capable of doing. That they wouldn't just throw me out to the wolves to fend for myself. Still, having to work in a Café, out front where I would actually have to deal with other people, was nerve-wracking. What if I went all mental again?

"Chad." Dion turned me around so I faced him fully. He slid his hand under my chin and tilted my head up, then he bent down and brushed his lips against mine.

My breath caught. This was the first kiss we'd shared since... well, I suppose we'd kissed that day I'd seduced him in the teacher's lounge. My memories were a bit fuzzy about that incident, as well as the weeks preceding. Still... He was kissing me, which was all I ever dreamt about, and it felt so good and so right and I never wanted to stop.

He did pull away, but he stroked his hand over my cheek in a loving sort of way and he smiled at me.

"Can we do this?" I whispered, afraid of the answer, but I had to know anyway.

"Of course we can. We've established that." He kissed me briefly again, drawing me in closer to himself now so our fronts pressed together.

"But ... Jeremy." I hated to put a damper on things, but I had to. Jeremy was a nice bloke, and I really did like him. "I know what you said he said, and he said to me, but nothing's happened, so I figured..." I shrugged.

"It's just a difficult transition." Dion brushed my hair out of my face. It was getting overly long. I should cut it soon—the minute I had money to actually pay to have it done properly.

"I suppose." I let it drop. I didn't want to keep rehashing it every time I felt anxious. Instead I got ready for work, and Dion walked with me down to the centre of Soho where the Café was situated.

I paused once we were outside it and stared in through the window. It seemed full, which scared the living hell out of me. My other jobs had mostly been as a busboy, working in the kitchen doing the dirty dishes. I hadn't had to deal with people—and I hadn't been able to hold the few jobs down for long anyway.

"You ready?" Dion's hand was heavy in my

shoulder again, like they'd been earlier when he'd pushed me down on the sofa to calm me down.

"No." I wasn't ready at all. But I knew I had to go in, there was no way around it. "Okay then. Let's do this."

Dion chuckled behind me, and then faithfully followed me inside as I opened the door. A bell above it jingled, and some of the customers turned to look at me. I shivered from the attention.

"Chad!" Harriet came round from the other side of the counter and she hugged me close.

"Hey." I hugged her back. I appreciated everything she did for me, even if it didn't seem like it whenever I was going mental.

"Jeremy!" Harriet bounced around the counter again, sticking her head in the kitchen door. "Can you watch out here for a bit while I show him the ropes?"

I didn't hear Jeremy's answers, but it must've been affirmative, because next I knew she was leading me into the break room.

Last time I'd been in the break room, I'd assaulted her girlfriend's son.

"We all have our own locker, if we want to keep a change of clothes. Accidents happen, so it's nice to have a set around if you're splashed full of coffee or milk or even water." She opened one of the lockers at the end of the line. "This one's yours. You can get a lock on it if you want."

"Okay." I felt I had to say *something*.

Harriet opened another locker and searched inside. "We don't have a particular uniform, but wearing plain black clothes is preferable. White is allowed, too, but black doesn't stain so easily. And we all wear aprons, again because it's easy to spill stuff and it's better to wash aprons every day than trousers."

She handed an apron over to me and I quickly tied it around my waist. *This is really happening.* I didn't feel ready, but after two weeks of nothing except going around the flat awkwardly, feeling like I didn't really belong in the middle of their lives, I had to do something with my time.

Harriet showed me the till and how to operate it, told me what my other responsibilities would be besides manning it, like cleaning the floor and wiping off tables and carrying dirty dishes into the kitchen and putting them in the washer.

The lunch rush was over, thankfully, so the Café was rather slow for my few hours. Once I was left to my own devices, while Harriet manned the counter out front, I escaped into the kitchen to say hi to Jeremy.

"You look good in that." He wore black trousers

and a white chef's shirt or whatever they were called, and the sentence just slipped out of me.

He smiled though, so I guess he didn't mind. "Thanks. You look good yourself."

Hardly. But I'd take the compliment.

"What're you doing?" I sidled up to him.

"Chopping vegetables. You wouldn't believe how many vegetables we use every day."

"The menu's that big?" I watched his fingers curl over an onion and how he swiftly chopped it up into pieces. "Doesn't chopping onion make you cry?"

"Used to before culinary school, but I've learned a few tricks since then. Besides, I chop it up so fast it hardly matters anyway."

"You'll have to teach me someday." Only when it was out did I realise it sounded like I planned to be around for a very long time. I hoped I could be, but I didn't want to put pressure on him. This must be just as awkward for Jeremy as it was for me.

Harriet called on me then, and it was back to duty.

The next three hours seemed to flow by as I cleaned up after people, tried my hand at the till and some customer service—and suddenly it was time to go home.

I met up with Jeremy in the break room, and it turned out he had the locker right next to mine. I smiled sheepishly as I squeezed past him to put my apron inside.

"Did you have a good day?" He smiled at me. "I think you did good, from what I saw."

"I think so. It wasn't as bad as I thought it'd be." Nothing ever really was it? Maybe I was just a very pessimistic person when my mood was stable. An extremely pessimistic person when I was depressed —but when I was manic everything was viewed in a positive light. *I miss it.*

I didn't voice that out loud. I had a feeling no one would like that admission.

"Ready to go?"

Jeremy's hand fluttered in my direction for a moment, but then he pulled it back. I gave an internal sigh, wishing he'd just *touch* me. If he did, maybe everything would feel so much better and so much easier instead of all this *hesitation*.

It all made me long for the high again, because then I'd just jump them both no matter what, thinking that of course they'd want me, *everyone* did. But that was the mania speaking, apparently, and not me. I didn't miss the crashes from high to low, but I sure did miss just the highs. They were so wonderful.

"Earth to Chad." Jeremy snapped his fingers in front of my face.

I jerked back, taken by surprise. "Sorry. Was just

thinking. But yeah, I'm ready to go." I grabbed my jacket and shrugged it on, then followed Jeremy outside.

"Bye, Harriet! See you in two days," Jeremy called into the kitchen, where Harriet was standing conversing with someone else. It was someone my age, a bloke with golden-brown hair and black-rimmed glasses I vaguely remembered having seen before. Well, at least I'd never done anything to *him*, so maybe one of my new coworkers wouldn't be hostile.

Not that I knew the others would be, but still... I would've been hostile if someone had done what I'd done.

"Chad, remember dinner tomorrow!" Harriet called after me, bringing me up short for a moment.

"Yeah," I replied, then slipped out the door Jeremy held open for me.

He was grinning. "You'd forgotten about it, hadn't you?"

"Well... Yeah." Dinner with Harriet and her girl-friend and her son. Last time I'd ended up in hospital before we'd even got that far, after assaulting said son and threatening another bloke who worked at the Café with a knife.

I didn't want another repeat of that, though now I was on medicine and my mood was mellow, so I doubted it would happen. Still, it *had* before and I couldn't bear for it to happen again. Not that aggressiveness. I didn't want to hurt anyone.

"Did I hurt you when I, well, *seduced* you?" Maybe I'd been forceful with him too, like I had been with Angelina's son. God, I couldn't even remember his *name.*

"Hurt me?" Jeremy seemed surprised at the question. "No. Not at all."

"Was it a bad experience, at least?"

"No, Chad. It wasn't." He stepped in close so our shoulders bumped together. "It was good."

"Would you want to do it again?" *No brain to mouth filter, I swear.* If this kept up, I was going to die of embarrassment some day soon.

Jeremy stared at me a moment. Maybe he was surprised at my straight-forwardness after these two weeks of silence—I sure was—or maybe the question itself surprised him. Maybe he *didn't* want to and didn't know how to put it nicely for me.

"Yeah." He nodded his head too. "I do."

I had to swallow the lump that suddenly stuck in my throat.

CHAPTER 2

*M*y heart was galloping.

Jeremy'd just admitted he *wanted* me. Or at least that he'd want a repeat of the wanking off session we'd had.

"But you want to take it slow?" He'd told me that too, back when I'd been in hospital.

"Yeah. It's just... I like to have a connection with my partner, you know. And we *do*, we do have a connection, but I don't feel like I know you all that well yet. I know you're sweet and troubled and broken, but most I've seen of you so far is the bipolar part, not the *you* part hiding underneath it."

"What about the last two weeks?" I couldn't help it, I *had* to dig.

"I feel like you've been avoiding me for the past two weeks." He cast me a sheepish look.

"Wha—I haven't!" How could he possibly think that? "I thought you felt awkward around *me*, so I tried to give you your space. I didn't mean to make you think—that wasn't my intention *at all*."

He stepped closer again, just short of our shoulders bumping this time. "I guess we have a case of bad communication. We should work on that."

"Yeah." I chuckled breathlessly.

His head tilted towards me. "I think we'll get there, in time."

"What kind of timeframe are you thinking?" I licked at my dry lips.

"I don't know."

At least he was honest. "Do you want me to stay away from Dion until then?" I didn't want to. I wanted to bury close to him and never let go. He was good, he was *mine*—mine and Jeremy's.

"No, I don't want that." He turned his head away now. "I see how good he is for you. Of course I don't want that."

I wanted to test the waters. I just hoped it wouldn't blow up in Dion's face. "We kissed earlier today. Do you mind that?"

He drew in a breath, and then coughed to clear

his throat. "No." I didn't quite believe him though. There was just something to his voice that told me he wasn't being completely honest.

"I will if that's what you want." I didn't want to ruin the chances of all three of us. If Jeremy needed time, I could keep my hands off Dion for the time-being. I could be a good lad.

"It's not. Not really. It's just... this whole three-some thing. I know I said I'm fine with it, but when it actually *comes* to it, I have no clue what to do."

"What do you mean?" I frowned up at him as I wrapped my arms around myself.

"Like, a relationship is hard enough to keep afloat when it's between two people. How are we supposed to do it if we're three? How are we supposed to sleep? How are we supposed to have *sex*? I've never been with more than one partner at once in my entire life. I've never so much as even thought about it." His hands moved around anxiously as he talked.

We were getting some strange looks from passers-by, but I wasn't sure if it was because of the hand-movements or if they heard the topic of our conversation.

"You've never had a threesome?"

"Have *you*?" He stared at me.

"Threesomes, foursomes, moresomes. You name

it, I've done it." How was it possible that someone went through their life, at least half-way through their twenties—though I didn't actually know how old Jeremy was—without sexual experimentation? "I've never had a relationship before, though. I do reckon you do it the same way as you do with one person, only with two."

"What if there's jealousy?" He wrung his hands in front of him, gaze darting around nervously. "I don't want to believe I will be, but if two of us spend more time together than with the third, then the third's going to feel left out."

"We'll just have to work on that, on not making anyone feel left out." In my mind it was so simple. Be together, have hot sex, sleep together, eat together, talk together... but then I knew nothing about relationships. And they'd been together for over two years. They had the relationship part down to a T, and now they were going to add me into it? It couldn't be easy for either of them.

"How does cuddling work with three people? It's not like three people can cuddle up on the sofa while watching the telly."

"Now you're just finding problems where there aren't any." Laughter escaped me, I couldn't help it. Jeremy was kind of cute when he fretted like this.

"Maybe." He buried his hands in his pockets and hunched his shoulders. "But it's new. It's... scary."

I didn't say anything to that. Everything was scary. I knew what was wrong with me, but that didn't make things any better. Now I didn't have the highs to look forward to, now I'd just have to settle for the middle-ground.

We got home, where Dion was sitting on the sofa with his feet propped up on the table and the laptop on his lap. He had earbuds in, but once he caught sight of us, he closed it with a snap.

"What were you watching?" Jeremy threw him a look as he headed towards the bathroom.

"Nothing, really."

Jeremy locked himself in the bathroom, while I sank down on the other sofa.

"How was your first day?"

"Okay, I guess." I couldn't complain anyway. It wasn't like it'd been *bad*. It'd just been something new, something I'd never done before, but with Jeremy and Harriet there it'd been okay. I wasn't looking forward to when they weren't going to be there though. The dread was settling heavy over me, making me feel all slow and heavy and drowsy. "I think I'm going to take a nap."

I stood before he could say anything and headed into the guest room, which had been *my* room for the past two weeks. Usually I minded, because I wanted to spend the night with one or both of them.

Right now, I was grateful to be alone as I lay down on the bed, fully dressed. I must've passed out immediately, because I couldn't remember anything else.

~

TAKING my medicine was a daily struggle.

The pills felt heavy in my palm and my hand trembled with the need to just drop them back down into their respective bottles, throw them in the sink, or flush them down the toilet. There wasn't a toilet in the bathroom, so that particular need was squelched, but the bottles were there and so was the sink.

If I put them back, I was sure they'd know, because they kept an eye on me. Both of them did.

If I let them flush down with the water in the sink, the evidence would be gone. Still, what if I went the wrong way if I quit taking them? What if I crashed instead of soared up high?

I didn't think anyone realised just what a struggle it was for me to medicate the part of me that I actually *liked*. I liked it when I was up high. I even liked the hallucinations when I had them, though when I crashed back down I always worried about my sanity. I knew what they were now though, so at least I knew I wasn't losing my mind completely. It was all just a part of my disorder. The one thing I'd inherited from my mum—besides my looks, anyway.

I took the pills, swallowing them down with a glass of water. I still almost choked on them, but that was no news. The pills were *big* and I hated taking pills in the first place.

I was up early, Dion and Jeremy hadn't risen yet when I finished in the bathroom, so I decided to go out for a walk.

The spring air was crisp and felt good against my skin, clearing my heavy head.

I headed over to Wynn's place, hoping against hope that he was home. I hadn't heard anything from him since I'd been admitted to hospital. All I knew was what Jeremy had told me—that Wynn had overdosed and was in hospital himself, and bound to stay for a bit.

There was no light on, at least as far as I could see from the street, and once I descended the stairs to bang on his door, there was no answer.

"Wynn." I wish he'd be home, that he'd open the door for me. I needed to see him, to talk to him. I needed to know he was *okay*. But there was no sounds from inside and no one opened the door.

I left, walking aimlessly around until I realised

which direction I was heading. I let myself continue, morbidly curious to go back there by myself.

Dad's house looked exactly the same as it had before. Before I'd been in the hospital, before he'd died, before I'd left him there without knowing he might've been dead at the time.

I had the key on my chain, so I unlocked the front door and headed inside. It smelled *foul*, but that didn't stop my slow exploration of the house I'd grown up in.

What a childhood it had been.

My eyes were drawn to the floor in front of the sofa, where Dion and Jeremy had said they'd found Dad. I walked over, but the only thing I could see were stains in the carpet. Those might've been there from earlier, from him binge-drinking or vomiting or from having his mates over.

Maybe it was sperm—maybe they'd wanked off together, because really, what kind of women would want their alcoholic, fat arses anywhere near them?

I remembered the mate who'd always creeped me out, the one I'd all but attacked during Dad's funeral. I wondered if his interest in me had been real or if it'd just been a figment of my mania. Had I been paranoid whenever it came to him? Very likely. But Dad and his mates had always been perverts, so I wouldn't put it past the ugly mug to actually do have an interest in me.

Wandering into the kitchen, my gaze instantly went to the floor in front of the sink. That was where I'd found my mum in a pool of blood. That was where I'd slipped and fallen in said blood and got it all over myself trying to wake her up. But she hadn't woken up, and Dad had been furious with me when he came home and realised she was gone.

No one had cleaned me up for hours.

I sunk to the floor, my back resting against the cabinet under the sink. Mum had slit her wrists here, ending her life. The floor had been covered in her blood. I couldn't count how many times my blood had been spilled on it afterwards, but it was many. He'd liked beating up on me in here. Maybe as punishment for not being able to save Mum.

"Why'd you do it, Mum?" I whispered to the room in general. "Why'd you leave me here alone with him?" I didn't know if it was true or not, but I had a suspicion Dad had been beating up on Mum long before she died. Long before he started in on me.

My breath stuttered in my throat. "I miss you."

I wished I could hear her voice, hear her tell me she loved me. I realised now it'd been her voice I'd heard that day I'd seduced Dion in the teacher's lounge. It hadn't been Dion telling me he loved me—because he didn't, as far as I knew—it had been *Mum*. I knew it was only hallucinations, that it wasn't really her, but I missed hearing it all the same.

Last time I'd heard voices, I'd heard Dad's too. That had not been pleasant. I could go for the rest of my life without hearing him in my head, but Mum… I missed her so much.

I wrapped my arms around my drawn-up knees and put my chin down on the top of them.

I didn't have a single good memory from this house. Mum had died here, Dad had died here—though that wasn't so much a bad memory as one of relief. Dad had beaten me up at least once in every single room, like he was going for the record.

He probably had been, the spiteful, old sod.

It wasn't a happy place, this house. Mum had given me the one thing that had made it bearable though—her bipolar disorder. At least, her mania. Without that, I would've done the same thing she had—slit my wrists and lain down to die right here on the kitchen floor.

What did I really have to live for anyway? My own dad had used me as his personal punching bag. Dion had chosen Jeremy over me, and though Jeremy said he was interested in all of us being together, I wasn't so sure he would go through with it if push came to shove.

And who would be left out, if it didn't work? That would be me.

It couldn't be anyone else.

CHAPTER 3

*D*inner was in a fancy restaurant I'd never even heard about before.

I suspected it had been Angelina's—Harriet's girl-friend's—doing. She was a posh solicitor, after all. She probably did fancy dinners with her clients all the time, and she probably used to take Harriet out to these kinds of places too.

They were already there; Harriet, Angelina, and Angelina's son. *What was his bloody name?* I couldn't for the life of me remember it.

"Chad!" Harriet jumped up to greet me, wrapping me in yet another of her tight hugs. She'd started doing that the past two weeks, after I'd been released from hospital, as if hugs could make up for everything that was shitty in my life. I couldn't lie though—the hugs were good, made me feel she actually cared for me. "I'm so glad you came."

"Didn't you think I would?" My gaze flickered nervously to Angelina's son, who sat with his head bowed. It seemed, judging from the chair Harriet had been sitting on, that I would be sitting next to her and opposite him.

"Of course I did." She smiled widely, but I had a feeling she was lying to me. *She didn't think I'd come.* But who could blame her? How many times had she asked me to dinner, and exactly how many times had I actually shown up? *None.*

"Hey, Chad." Angelina thrust her hand out, and I shook it after a moment's hesitation. I didn't know if her serious face was the way she always was, or if she didn't like me very much for what I'd done to her son. "I don't think you've met Joshua properly, my son." She motioned to him.

Josh. The name popped into my brain then, even if she used his full name. The lad in question finally lifted his head, his gaze flickering a bit as he looked at me.

"Hey." I slunk over to sit on the only available chair.

"Hey." His voice was low, unsure.

"Look, I'm sorry," I said quickly, before I would

regret it or mess it up. "For what I did. I'm really sorry."

He blinked down at the table. "It's okay. I know it wasn't you, really. A girl in my group is bipolar, so I know a bit about what it's like."

"Group?" I frowned.

His green eyes were wide as he looked up again. "Group therapy?"

"Oh, right." Of course. *Obviously.* I'd had group therapy in the hospital. They wanted me to keep it up now I was out of hospital, but I needed to actually get comfortable with my psychiatrist first. Then, perhaps, I could progress to a group of strangers.

We settled into uncomfortable silence, in which I gladly buried myself behind my menu. Only to find I could hardly understand it. "What is this?"

"What'd you mean?" Harriet bent over to me.

"I can't read this." I put it back down on the table.

Angelina's gaze settled on me. "It's French. But with English descriptions underneath."

I picked the menu up again hesitantly, and indeed she was right. That didn't mean the English was any easier for me to figure out. I got stuck on every single word that had four or more letters.

Maybe Dion's right. Maybe I should get tested for dyslexia.

I hadn't had to deal with taking orders in the Café yesterday, but now that I thought about it, it would be a big part of the job. And here I was, almost unable to read anything, least of all write it down in something that was understandable for someone else.

Oh my God. I can't do this job. I'm going to fail.

My breathing started to get more laboured by the second, and it stuttered to a halt completely for a second when a waiter appeared right next to me out of the blue.

It did stop me from freaking out entirely, which I reckoned was a good thing. On the other hand, I hadn't even finished reading the first thing on the menu, so I had no idea what they had to offer.

Only drinks were ordered now though, so it gave me a little while still to try and puzzle out the menu.

"Harriet," I mumbled after a while, frustrated to the point of tears.

"Yes, love?" She turned to me with a smile, but it fell when she actually had a good look at me.

"I can't read this. Any of it," I admitted in a low voice. "I can't read and I can't write in a way that people understand. I can't do my job at the Café."

"What do you mean you can't?" Her eyebrows drew together in a frown.

"Dion seems to think I might have dyslexia." It

was a better alternative than to just be plain stupid, wasn't it?

"Have you been tested?"

I shook my head. "No. I didn't want to be. I quit college instead." And because Dion had chosen Jeremy over me, but she didn't need to know that. Also because I'd needed a job, which I'd been able to hold for a couple of weeks before Dad beat the crap out of me, causing me to miss it. It had landed me in Jeremy's arms though—literally—so I couldn't really complain about the outcome.

"You have to get tested, Chad." She thought for a moment. "How'd you manage to pass your GCSEs on the second try?"

"I broke my hand before taking them, so they allowed me to use a computer. They've got spelling programmes." It was the only reason I'd passed them. I'd managed to fail spectacularly on my first try, and barely passed on the second. But I'd had another year of studying to do for them too, another year of school, so I'd figuratively had it beaten into my skull by repetition.

Harriet cleared her throat. "I remember when you did that. You said you tripped down the stairs."

There was a question attached to that statement. I could hear it loud and clear. "I might've had some help on the trip down said stairs." She knew Dad was an abusive sack of shit now, so why continue to lie to her?

She drew in a deep breath as her unasked question was answered.

I could feel two pairs of eyes to me, and when I turned my head back properly Josh quickly bowed his head, but Angelina kept her gaze steady on me. It was a bit unnerving. No, it was *a lot* unnerving.

The waiter came back with drinks and everyone but me was ready to order. Josh ordered something meaty, so I ordered the same. I had no idea what Harriet and Angelina had ordered, as they'd just said the number of the dish.

"How's college going, Josh?" Harriet turned her smile on Josh, who seemed startled at being addressed. I was pretty sure his attention had been on me, because his eyes flickered guiltily from side to side.

"Oh, it's okay. I've only got college to focus on now, so it's rather easy actually. Damian helps me study when he can too, but he's very busy."

"Yeah, med-school isn't exactly something he can slack on."

Med school? My eyebrows inched up my forehead. *Josh's boyfriend must be real smart.*

"I think he likes the challenge." Josh smiled sheepishly. "He's always known what he wanted to be. He's focused and driven. Quite different from some of us." By some of us he clearly meant himself.

Though it applied to me too. What the hell was I going to do with my life? I couldn't read or write properly, I had no proper education. I wasn't good for anything. *What the hell do Dion and Jeremy even see in me? Why do they keep me around?*

Depression had been over me all day, but now it felt like it pushed me down and choked me. I heard them keep a conversation in the background, but the words flew by me. The words didn't matter. What did matter was that I was a major mess of a human being, and why would anyone want to keep me around?

"I need some air." I pushed away from the table and all but ran outside without even hearing what they had to say to it.

Once outside I gulped in the crisp air. A light drizzle had started while I'd been inside, but it wasn't enough to drench me through.

"Are you okay?"

I whirled around to face Josh. "Yes!" It came out too quickly, too loudly, and too obviously a lie.

He stared at me. "Isn't your medicine working?"

"Wha—I don't know. Yes. Yes, it is." Of course it was. If it wasn't working, I'd be rapid cycling like mad. I wouldn't have stayed in a normal mood for two bloody weeks if the medicine hadn't been working. "Why are you in therapy?" I needed to get the subject off of me.

"I've got Borderline Personality Disorder." He said it earnestly, like it was just a state of fact. Maybe it was, to him, maybe he'd known about his mental illness, or whatever it was, for a very long time.

"I don't know what that is."

"It's a mood disorder, just like bipolar, where I've got an inability to control my emotions. I don't fluctuate between depression and mania, and I certainly don't have psychosis, but they're both mood disorders and it makes my mind a mess sometimes. A lot of times." He kicked his feet awkwardly. "Just ask my boyfriend. He's the one who has to live with me."

"How does he cope?" It slipped out, like things tended to do with me. I hadn't meant for it to sound so harsh, like it was a burden to the boyfriend, because it might not be. "I mean, how does he deal with it?" I wasn't sure that was any better phrasing.

"He's the most patient person ever. And he loves me."

"You're lucky." I wrapped my arms around myself, the drizzle starting to get to me. "To have someone like that, I mean."

"Harriet says you've got two someones."

I was taken aback. "When did she say that?"

He shrugged. "A while ago now."

"I don't. Not really. I mean we're not together or anything." *Oh, how I wish this was untrue.* It might be in the future, but as of right now... things were just awkward. "It's nothing really."

"Okay." He seemed willing to take my word for it. He was so bloody earnest about it.

"I really am sorry for what I did. I know it's not an excuse, but when I'm like that I think everyone wants me. Like, how could they not? So when you were saying no I was just thinking you were playing hard to get, because sex is something everyone wants, but I know it's not and I'm really sorry." I stopped to take a breath.

"It's okay. Truthfully, it helped me get some perspective over my own wants and needs."

I eyed him dubiously. "I appreciate you saying that, but still..."

"No, I mean it. It's true. I was all hung up on sex that day, but after you, well... I realised I didn't really want it, not now at least, and that I wasn't ready to have it again anyway. It's all good." He smiled.

I was lost. "It's good... that you don't want *sex*?"

"Yeah." He nodded, as if that was a perfectly normal thing.

It wasn't.

Who didn't want sex? I always wanted it, though

not to the extreme I did when I was manic and hypersexual. *That's what they call it, apparently.*

"Are you ready to come back in? I think the food must've arrived by now." He motioned back towards the door.

Well, I wasn't feeling like I couldn't breathe anymore, at least. "Yeah, okay." The quicker I ate, the quicker I could get it done. I just wanted to get home and go to bed.

Though I'd been AWOL all day, so that wasn't a very likely scenario to happen. At least not instantly. Though they didn't have to worry anymore, did they? It wasn't like I could get manic now I was on antipsychotic, which meant I wouldn't go out and do anything stupid.

Okay, doing something stupid was kind of my life, but at least I wouldn't go out and do something *dangerous*. Like jump from a bridge or Wynn's balcony. *And all the other dangerous things I've done through the years.*

Now I was on medicine, I was calm and *mellow* and *anxious*. And I missed the highs. I missed them so much.

I wish they'd come back.

CHAPTER 4

I heard someone move around the flat Monday morning, then leave.

I stretched languidly in the bed, and then rolled out of it. I padded barefoot over to the door and to the bathroom, not expecting anyone else to be up now that Dion had headed off to work.

Only when I opened the bathroom door, I was met with the sight of Dion clad only in his boxers—and my morning wood, which I hadn't even given a thought to, was now begging for attention.

I stood there gaping, frozen in place, and it seemed he was too, because for a whole minute all he did was stare back at me.

Then his eyes dropped to my crotch—and as I

was only wearing boxers too, he had no trouble seeing exactly how excited the sight of him made me.

My own gaze dropped down his mostly naked body and—*yes!*—he was hardening up fast. I did a mental fist bump, then I stepped further into the room without a second thought. The evidence was right there—that he wanted me.

He turned fully, then grabbed for me, and I fell in against him, answering the kiss with passion. We didn't say a word, our bodies did all the talking as our hard cocks lined up together.

He grabbed me under my arse, lifted me and turned us both around, then put me down on the counter. I wrapped my legs around his hips, holding him there against me.

It was frantic. I felt like I'd been starving for weeks—and maybe he did too. He sure was just as frantic as I was, and it didn't take us long to chuck the one piece of clothing we both wore and get down to the dirty.

He must've had lube within reach, because soon he pushed inside of me, and I spread my legs wider to accommodate him. I was out of practice when it came to sex by now, and my thighs burned, but the feel of him inside, of him thrusting into my body, was so good it triumphed it.

I panted and moaned, unintelligible sounds

leaving me. My arms clutched at his shoulder, scratching lightly before I got a good grip.

He bucked against me, groaning, hands in a bruising grip on my arse-cheeks.

There were times I could come from penetration alone. This was one of those times, and I cried out and arched my back as I shot over his stomach.

He grunted, hips stuttering for a moment before gaining even more speed. He continued fucking me until I didn't know which was up and which way was down, and when he did falter to a stop and pulled out, I felt like melting to goo at his feet.

I didn't do anything quite so drastic, but I leant back so my shoulder blades rested against the cold mirror. I pulled both knees up to brace myself against the counter so I wouldn't fall off in an embarrassing heap, and it was then I felt it trickle out of me.

He came inside me.

And then a realisation: *he fucked me bare.*

Letting my gaze drop, I took in his heaving chest as he gathered himself, and then down to his cock, softening by the second and glistening with lube and semen.

"Oh my God." It deserved that sentiment. It really, *really* did. That must've been the best sex I'd ever had while in a normal, moderate mood.

His eyes were locked on my lower body. More specifically on his bodily fluids trickling out of me.

"Fuck." He ran a hand through his coarse hair, then strode forward and crushed himself to me, lips finding mine in a hard, hot kiss. "I need a shower." He only pulled back far enough once he ended the kiss so he could look down at me. "Come in with me?"

My chest squeezed in utter happiness. "Yes!" *He wants me. Oh God oh God oh God.*

I was already hard again by the time we were under the water.

"To be young again," he laughed, stroking me once before turning to adjust the heat.

"Oh, come on, you're not exactly *old*." I pressed up against his back, the head of my cock butting up against the underside of his arse, while I scattered kisses all over his back. "You're fucking gorgeous naked. I didn't see you naked that day in college, but I felt all these muscles." I felt them now too, with no clothes in-between our skin. "So hot."

He turned around, and I let my arms run over him as he did, only to wrap around his torso once we were face to face.

"You've got no idea how long I've dreamt of this." I stared up at him.

"Since the first time you saw me in the classroom.

Wasn't that what you said?" He carded my hair away from my cheeks, while him being taller shielded me from getting the shower spray directly in the face. "I can't say I wanted *you* from the first time I saw you, because that would be a lie. But you grew on me, slowly but surely. To the point I cheated on my own boyfriend with you."

The mention of Jeremy felt like I'd taken an ice-cold shower, instead of being inside a rather hot one. "Is he working double shifts today?" Because I had heard someone leaving, and he was supposed to work the late shift at the Café with me.

"Yeah."

"What's he going to say about this? Is he going to be mad?" He wanted us to go slow. I suppose that meant all three of us, and shagging bareback in the bathroom was not the definition of taking things slow.

I didn't want to make Jeremy feel bad—but when it came to sex, my mind wasn't exactly of sound mind. Once the possibility was on the horizon, everything else flew by the wayside to be replaced with thoughts of *sex, sex, sex.*

"Jeremy's the one who suggested this in the first place."

"Me and you shagging?" I had a hard time believing that.

"All three of us. But he also said that if that didn't work, I could still be with you. And with him. I hope that's okay with you?"

I nodded quickly. Of course that was okay with me. Everything to be with him. But the thought of things not working out with Jeremy made me extremely disappointed. He was a handsome, caring bloke and I did like him, even if I didn't know him as well as I knew Dion.

"Turn around." He gently guided me around to face the wall, and I let him do it willingly without knowing what he had planned. "Time to clean you up." I'd expected hands and soap on skin, but his index fingers breached my hole instead and I lurched forward to catch myself against the wall.

A low, drawn-out moan escaped from my throat. "First time I saw you, you were standing in front of the class, introducing yourself," I forced out through the pleasure of his finger in my arse. I was a sucker for *anything* in my arse. Nothing turned me on more.

"First time I saw you, you came shuffling in too late with bruises on your face. You were hunched over in this big hooded jumper, so I'm pretty sure you had bruises other places too."

"Y-yeah." My eyes closed and my cheek rested against the wall too, mouth hanging open in pleasure as he thrust two fingers inside me. "Had a fight with

Dad. You asked me to stay back after class. You asked me if I was okay."

"You assured me you were." With a slight curve of his fingers he hit that sweet spot, and I nearly unravelled. He had to wrap his other arm around my thighs to keep me standing. "And since you didn't want to tell the truth, there was nothing I could do."

"You kept trying." He'd kept me back after almost every English class. And I'd always found an excuse to *not* leave the classroom as quickly as I used to. I always hoped he would ask me to stay, that he would show his normal concern, that he'd touch my hand.

So innocent, to want him to touch my hand.

Of course, I'd dreamt of more—a lot more—but I'd been realistic. I'd known it wouldn't happen.

Until something changed. Maybe it'd been me and my mania that had seen something that he had kept hidden, but I had jumped him and he had responded. And now here we were, naked and in the shower together, with him playing with my arse. My biggest turn-on. My dick was already leaking.

"I fell so fast and so hard for you," I moaned. He'd been the only teacher to show any real concern. The others mostly ignored me, like I didn't matter to them. But I had to him—since that very first day. And I would *never* forget that. "You were the only good thing about college."

"Then why didn't you ever tell me the truth?" He withdrew his fingers and I genuinely felt the loss.

"I couldn't. Dad and the house was all I had. I couldn't have that taken away from me. I couldn't live on the streets. I was over eighteen, so it wasn't like I could go into foster care."

I made to push myself out from the wall, but then Dion was back in close to me, but not with his finger this time. His *tongue* licked over my hole and I nearly lost it then and there. He licked again, three times, and then pressed it past the tight ring of muscles.

"*Oh my God!*" I hit the wall with clenched fists, my feet trembling. He still had a strong arm wrapped around my thigh, but not even that could keep me up now. I fell in a tangle into his lap, as he was kneeling.

"I love anal," he whispered in my ear, cradling me close. "Jeremy doesn't though."

"You bottom?" That surprised me. I'd always thought of him as the ultimate top. Maybe because he was so much bigger than me, or so much older. I wasn't sure.

"Oh, no. I can't stand *that*. Neither of us likes to be fucked, so it's not often we have anal sex. We stick to other things." His fingers were back in my crack now, and I tilted my arse further in to meet them. I needed something inside me *now*.

"I love anal. Anal alone makes me come, you

won't even have to touch my cock." I gripped his neck, desperate for something more. When his fingers finally did slip inside me, I rode them like I'd ride his cock, if it had been hard. "I wish all three of us could do this. How hot would that be? You could both fuck me. At the same time. Double-fuck me."

He groaned, his forehead dropping to my shoulder. "Don't say things like that."

"Why not?" I rode his fingers like a fiend now, my orgasm *so close*. "You don't think it would be any good?"

"Too good." He nipped at my shoulder and that was *it*—I came with a loud cry I'm sure the neighbours had to hear. "There's nothing I want more than for all three of us to be together and comfortable and happy."

I was coming down from the high the orgasm gave me and I turned around to straddle his lap. The hot water from the shower beat down on me now, but I peered at him through the water. "I want that too. I think we could be so good together." Though I still didn't really know what they saw in me. "I've been thinking."

"About what?" His lips brushed over my jaw and cheek.

"Maybe I should get tested for dyslexia, after all."

Better to have another diagnosis on board, I suppose. At least then I had a reason for being so stupid.

"What about college?" His lips brushed my ear now.

"Don't know." I didn't want to give that any thoughts yet. "I can't go back to yours anyway, seeing as we're a lot more than simple teacher and student now. Wouldn't want to get you fired."

"There are lots of colleges to choose from." His hands ran up my sides.

"There's months still until a new school year starts." I had time. Lots of time to think. There was absolutely no hurry. "I'll think about it. I promise."

He kissed me again, but softer this time, and a lot more chaste as there was no tongue. Simply lips on lips. It was just as good as the passionate ones. "That's good. Now let's get cleaned up before the water goes cold."

It was just as well we had no more sexual distractions, as it didn't take long for the hot water to run out. We must've been busy for quite a while.

Still, I'd take a bit of cold water as long as I could have him.

CHAPTER 5

"**W**ynn?"

I was back knocking on his door, hoping once again that he'd come home. But like it had been for the past two weeks, there was no answer.

Turning to leave, I hesitated, deciding on a whim to try the knob. Jeremy had told me that trying the knob when he'd been here last was the only reason he'd found Wynn overdosed on the sofa. That if he'd left without trying it, Wynn likely would've died.

I hadn't expected the knob to turn—but it did, and I was faced with a dark hole in front of me. A ball of fear dropped right into my stomach and it bounced wildly.

The flat was pitch black. All curtains were drawn,

no lights to be seen. My heart beat wildly as I flicked on the light right inside the front door. I was afraid I'd see Wynn on the sofa, overdosed on drugs like Jeremy had found him weeks ago, but the sofa was empty.

"Wynn?" I stepped in and closed the door. The flat smelled closed off, like it hadn't been aired out or cleaned for a long time.

Jeremy'd said he'd opened the windows to air out the smell of vomit when he'd left, but that'd been weeks ago now. With the curtains drawn and the windows shut, it meant someone had been here. And Wynn didn't have anyone in his life who gave a shit about him, so it could only be him.

I walked slowly to the bedroom, dread settling heavy in my gut.

What would I find once I pushed that door open? I was afraid to find out, but at the same time I had to, so I put my palm to it and gently pushed it open.

There was a big lump on the bed, illuminated now by the light behind me. Duvets, pillows—and Wynn, curled up in the middle of it all.

"Wynn?" Had he taken drugs here? Had he passed out? Was he *dead*?

I walked over, my breath stuttering from fright, but then I saw his shoulders rise and fall. *He's alive.*

"Wynn?" I shook said shoulder.

"Go away," he rasped.

Relief was sudden and all-consuming. If he could talk, he surely hadn't overdosed on anything again. I couldn't see any drugs in the near facility either, unless he had it buried up on the bed with him.

"Wynn, please. I've been so worried about you."

"Leave me alone." He moved slightly to bury his face in the duvet, which was bunched around him.

"Why didn't you ring me when you came out? I've been so worried about you." He must've taken something, since he was just lying there. This wasn't like Wynn—not like I knew him. "Wynn?"

"Go." His voice was still raspy, like it hadn't been used for a long time.

The closed-off smell was worse in here. "How long have you been lying like this?"

No answer.

"Days? Weeks?"

Still no answer. No movement at all.

"Wynn?" I tried to search the bed around him, but didn't come up with any drugs. So instead I headed into the bathroom to check there, as the coffee table in the living room had been clean as well.

The bathroom was a mess, clothes and towels tossed about. Was this from now though, or from before he'd been in hospital?

This is where Madison died.

The thought struck me suddenly and I snatched for breath.

Madison.

I hadn't given him much thought lately. He hadn't been a *close* friend of mine, he'd been too odd to get to know properly, but he'd been the closest person to Wynn.

I opened the cabinets, just to see if there was something of note in there, and... I was met with a handful of prescription bottles.

"Wynn? What's this?"

I tried to read the bottles, but the names on them were too long and too complicated for me. I didn't think I'd recognise anyone if I had been able to read them either.

Though there was one... *P-r-o-z—* "Prozac?" I knew that one! Back in hospital, it'd been used as an example of the type of tablets I couldn't take, as they would likely induce my mania.

I strode over to the doorway. "Why do you have antidepressants? Wynn?"

"Just leave me alone," he groaned, burying further into his fort of duvets and pillows.

"How long have you been on them? There's a handful of prescriptions in there." I didn't know if all of them were antidepressants, only the one I recognised, but what else could they be? "Why have you been hiding this from me? *Wynn?*"

It was impossible to get an answer.

"Why did you stop taking them?" Because obviously he had, or else he wouldn't have been lying listlessly in bed for days, possibly weeks. Though at that, it couldn't have been weeks, could it? He would need food and drink, at least. "Can you take them now, please?" My voice shook. "Wynn, please."

He'd been my best mate for years. How come I hadn't known he was depressed?

Had Madison known?

He probably had, he'd known everything about Wynn—and yet still he'd left him.

I hated Madison right then, because even though Wynn liked to think he could manage everything himself, that he could be by himself—Madison had been his world and losing him had caused Wynn to crash and burn.

Wynn had done his own *drugs* for god's sake, and he *never* did drugs. He didn't have anything against giving me or Madison drugs, but he'd always been against them himself, besides selling them anyway.

Maybe if he'd been depressed for years and on medicine for it… maybe drugs would interfere with that as well? They would for me certainly, I'd been told again and again in the hospital. Still, if I was presented with some, I wasn't sure what I'd do. All they did was induce the mania, which was the good, the *happy*, part. The part I liked. The part I *missed*.

A look at the watch on my phone told me I should get going.

"I have to get to work, Wynn, but I'll be back once I'm done, okay?" I scooped all the prescription bottles out of the cabinet. Now I'd made him aware of them, I didn't want to come back and find he'd swallowed them all.

Maybe Jeremy would make some food for me to bring too? It didn't hurt to ask, anyway. If he didn't, I'd have to get something together. I was sure Harriet wouldn't mind—she could take it from my pay-check in any case.

"I'll be back, I promise."

No answer, no movement.

Shit, this is bad. This was *me*, when I was so far down I couldn't get out of bed. Had he suffered from the same this whole time?

No, not the same. Wynn wasn't bipolar. He was on antidepressants, which told me he was depressed. No doctors would prescribe antidepressants to someone with bipolar—at least they hadn't wanted to me.

"Don't lock me out, Wynn!"

I caught sight of his keys on the table next to the door on my way out—so I snagged them. I couldn't take the chance. I knew what I was like when I was so far down, and I didn't for a second believe he had any different thoughts than I did.

Whereas I didn't have the energy to move when I was like that, least of all act on all my thoughts of suicide, I wasn't sure if he would or not. Act on it, that was.

So I pocketed the keys and headed off to work, hoping the few hours until closing would go by in a flash.

"How was your second day?" Jeremy asked when I turned the lock on the door.

He helped me turn the chairs over and put them up on the tables, which was nice of him, considering his job was to clean the kitchen. I'd help him with that afterwards.

"It was okay." Considering I'd spent the four hours I'd been there in a state of constant worry, I couldn't really remember what exactly I'd been doing. It was like I'd been going on auto-pilot. I was sure I'd done a ton of mistakes. There hadn't been a lot of people though, so hopefully I'd managed okay.

"You've been distracted."

Maybe not so okay. "It's been very noticeable?"

Of course it had been, as I couldn't even remember most of the things I'd been doing for all the worrying.

"Yeah." He smiled. "Are you all right?"

"Yeah, I'm fine." I'd never been better, truthfully. Most of it was because of the medicine, but also because of Dion. Because of what we'd been doing early that morning. And we'd spent the rest of the day together before I'd headed over to Wynn's. "Turns out Wynn's been home for a while. I don't know for how long."

"He wouldn't tell you?" Jeremy turned the last chair over.

"He wouldn't tell me anything. He was... he was like I use to be, when I've crashed from a high. He was just lying in bed, not moving, hardly speaking besides telling me to leave him alone. And I found prescription medicine in his cabinet, and I recognised one. It was Prozac. So he *is* depressed, and he's been medicated for it too—but he's still just lying there and I don't know what to do."

"What did you do when you were there?" Jeremy leaned back against the counter to look at me.

"Nothing. I hadn't expected him to be home, so I had to go if I wanted to be punctual for work. But I brought all his medicine with me, just in case. And his keys."

I patted my sides, even though I knew I didn't have any pockets on my T-shirt.

"Where are they now?"

"In my jacket. In my locker." I crossed my arms over my chest and hunched over a bit. "I'd hoped you could maybe fix some food? I think he's been lying like that for days. I have to go back and check on him. I was thinking I'd maybe spend the night there, just to make sure he doesn't do anything drastic. And to make him see that he still has *someone*."

"That's very kind of you." Jeremy nodded. "I can heat up some soup and make a few sandwiches. Maybe a salad too? With pasta. He needs carbs for energy."

"Yeah, that sounds great." I trailed after him into the kitchen.

"Did he open the door for you this time? You've been over there every day, without any sign of life."

"No, I—I thought about you, about you trying the knob when I asked you to go over and check on him, and it was open. I found him curled up in bed, under a pile of duvets and pillows, in total darkness." I wrung my hands as I sat down on the stool that was placed in the kitchen. "What do you think I should do if he doesn't improve? Should I ring for an ambulance?"

"If he's so depressed he can't move or can't eat, so

much he can't take proper care of himself, then he's a danger to himself and they can section him."

Hospital. Again. Wynn had just got out after his overdose.

"But he has medicine."

"Doesn't matter if he doesn't want to take it." Jeremy was chopping away now, salad, onion, chicken, tomato, you name it. Soup was already stewing on the cooker.

It didn't take him long to finish off making the food, and he even put it into containers and a bag for me to carry it in, while I started cleaning up. We worked in silence, cleaning down the kitchen, and then we headed into the back room to get out of our aprons and into our jackets.

"Thanks so much for this." I looked up at him once we were outside and the door was safely locked.

"It wasn't any trouble." He buried his hands in his pockets.

"Your shift was over. You weren't required to. You could've gone home."

"I really couldn't have." His gaze was intense. "Not when it's you asking."

The atmosphere was loaded between us, and it felt like something was about to happen.

Though I had the feeling, I was the one who actually did something. I stepped closer to him, into his personal bubble, and then tilted my head up just as he tipped his down.

The kiss was slow, hesitant, but his lips were soft and warm.

"Take care, okay?" he said when he pulled back. "If you need anything, anything at all, don't hesitate to ring us."

His words warmed and I felt a wide smile split my lips. I kissed him one more time, a quick press of lips, then took several steps away, in the direction I had to go.

He stared at me.

I lifted my hand in a wave. "Be back tomorrow." *Hopefully.* If I could leave Wynn.

He lifted his hand in a wave too, then he set down the street in the opposite direction from me.

Once I turned the corner ahead, I jumped in the air and did a fist-pump. "*Yes!*"

He'd kissed me of his own free will. That was promising.

Maybe we could figure things out anyway.

And that thought was *wonderful.*

PART II
DION

CHAPTER 6

I was on the laptop when I heard the door open.

The sound was on tonight, as I hadn't bothered getting my earbuds, and the moans seemed loud to my ears. I quickly clicked pause, then snapped the screen closed—just as Jeremy stepped into the flat.

"Where's Chad?" I frowned, expecting Chad's auburn hair to appear behind him, but it didn't. Instead Jeremy closed the door, which he certainly wouldn't have done if Chad had been with him.

"It seems Wynn's been home for days." Jeremy shrugged out of his jacket and put his shoes away, then came over to sink down on the sofa next to me. "He's depressed. And I'm speaking depressed to the point of not-being-able-to-get-out-of-bed depressed.

Chad went to spend the night with him, make sure he didn't do anything stupid."

Chad spending the night with his drug-dealing best friend worried me, but *his* worry was also endearing. "He's a good lad."

"He is." Jeremy's eyes went to the laptop covering my lap. "What've you been up to?"

"Oh, nothing much." I couldn't put the laptop away, or he'd know something was definitely *up*.

"You mind if I check something?"

"Uh." *Well, shit.*

He eyed me. "I'll go take a shower while you shut down whatever it is you've been doing." He pushed himself back up and disappeared into the bathroom.

I tilted my head back to rest against the sofa as I listened to the shower start up. When I was certain he wouldn't come back out, I opened the laptop again. The video I'd been watching was frozen in front of me in a very compromising picture. I shut it down and dropped the laptop to the side, then pressed the palm of my hand against my groin, trying to get my hard cock to deflate on its own without a helping hand.

It felt wrong somehow to watch porn when I had a perfect boyfriend—and Chad, whatever I was going to call him. Speaking of which, guilt gnawed at me about this morning. I didn't regret it, per say, because I desired Chad so bloody much—but while Jeremy said he was okay with it, I wasn't sure he would be if once again faced with the knowledge that I'd shagged someone who wasn't him.

It didn't take long for the shower to turn off—and I steeled myself, debating how to bring the subject up. I felt like I had back when I'd had to come home and tell Jeremy I'd cheated on him. Like I was a cheater. I wasn't *really*. I wasn't like my father. But falling in love with two people… well, that wasn't like him, because he didn't love anyone—he never had.

Still. Having sex with two different people when they weren't having sex with each other felt *wrong*. Like I was cheating them both. And also like I had the good deal in these two relationships, while they had to settle for seconds.

"Want to tell me what you were looking at now?" Jeremy came out of the bathroom in joggers and a T-shirt, drying his hair with a towel before drawing it over his shoulder as he sat down next to me again. He drew the laptop onto his lap and started typing on it.

"Porn." It slipped out. I didn't want to talk to him about my newly acquired porn habits—I needed to talk to him about Chad. Again. I felt like that was the only thing we *did* talk about lately.

He threw me a shrewd look. "And you didn't want to say anything because—?"

"Threesome porn." I met his gaze, trying not to sound and be too ashamed. With them not being a thing, it didn't feel right. "For research."

Jeremy's lips parted a fraction, then he cleared his throat and bent over the laptop. "I kissed him earlier. It was nice. Well, okay, that's not the most descriptive verb. It was *good*. *Great* even."

"That's... good." It was. It really was. I wanted them to get along, to *move along*. The quicker they did, the quicker we could all figure out our place in the mess I'd made of all of our lives. Because if I hadn't given into Chad that day, we probably wouldn't have been here now.

"It was." He nodded, but kept his gaze on the keyboard. "He really is a sweet, mild-mannered and handsome lad."

I had to say it. "I had sex with him this morning." Straight out with it, no hedging, no hinting. It was better that way.

Jeremy stilled. "All right."

"Is it?" I watched him anxiously.

"We've already talked about it." He sighed. "We've talked it to death."

"Doesn't mean I don't worry. I don't want to hurt you."

He licked his lips. "I agreed to this."

"That doesn't mean you can't be hurt." If we could just get the whole threesome relationship started, this would be so much easier. Then they could be together too, instead of it being just me wanting to have my cake and eating it at the same time. "If you regret it, Jem, you have to tell me. Whatever it is, you have to tell me."

"I don't regret anything. I just... I don't know how to start it." He was still typing on the laptop, intent on whatever it was he saw on the screen.

"Me neither. That's why I've been doing... well, I guess you can call it research." I reckoned more people than me had called porn research. It wasn't like I'd never watched if before, of course I had, but I'd never watched threesome porn, like I did now. It had never been of any interest—except now I figured I had two boyfriends, so now it was a major part of my life.

He cast me a look again. "Threesome porn, huh? Was it hot?"

I couldn't possibly lie. "Yeah. It was hot." My cock was still hard, for god's sakes. Only my hands resting in my lap kept it from making a tent of my trousers.

Jeremy's gaze dropped to my lap though, and by the slight press of his lips I reckoned he knew exactly what kind of problem I had. "Why don't you show me what you've been watching?"

"Now?"

"Now's a good as time as any." He made a final click on the touchpad, then dropped the laptop back on my lap. "I need to do the research too, I suppose. I've got no idea what we're going to do. I mean, sex is sex and all, but I've never had a threesome. What do you do with three dicks and three pairs of arms and legs? I imagine it'll be awkward."

"Actually, no." I typed in the URL to the porn site I'd found the best amateur porn on. The amateur stuff was best, as that was what we were. *Amateurs.* "This one for example." I found one of the ones I'd watched several times. They weren't full videos, as I didn't have a subscription, but clips put together from what I assumed at least to be a longer one.

Jeremy leaned in close to me, the smell of soap and his shampoo washing over me. "One lad fucking the other while being fucked by the third?" He pursed his lips.

"Give it a moment." That wasn't an ideal position. Neither Jeremy nor I particularly liked to be penetrated. "*This* could be possible." The scene had changed now.

"What are they—" Jeremy drew in a breath as the third partner climbed over the thighs of the one on the bottom, then pressed his hard cock inside the man riding the first one. It slipped in easily, so either the man taking them both was used to it, or they'd used a shit-ton of lube.

The bottom man stopped his movements, and now only the second one was doing the fucking. But all three of them were moaning out loud, so it must still be just as good for him as if he'd been moving.

"Chad proposed it this morning." I slid one palm over to Jeremy's thigh. "He said he loved being fucked—and that since we didn't, we were free to double-fuck him. Not his exact words, as I can't remember them, but that was the gist of it."

"Okay. That…" Jeremy's eyes followed the movements on screen, and as the camera zoomed in we got an eyeful of it. "… is hot."

I felt his groin, and as expected he was hardening right up. "I know, right?" I massaged him through his joggers, loving the feel of him growing harder underneath my palm. "It's not so hard, three men having sex."

"If we all get together…" He leaned further into me, his voice turning slightly breathless as I continued to massage him. "Should we have rules? Can we have sex whenever we want, or should all three be in on it?"

I shrugged. "Depends on what we're all fine

with." One of the men had come inside the bottom partner, and semen dripped down the cock of the one lying on his back.

The third partner pulled out now and preceded to lick the come off of both of the other two. He even went so far as to thrust his tongue inside, while the partner lying down was still thrust deep inside him.

Jeremy pulled back a bit with a grimace. He wasn't big on arseplay at all—neither penetrative nor by using tongue back there.

"Okay, that squicks me out a bit. Really. I hope he cleaned out."

A chuckle escaped me. "I'm sure he did. It is porn after all. Wouldn't make a very good porn film if he hadn't." The clip ended and I searched up another of my favourites. "This one's different, but just as hot."

There were three lads, obviously, and one was on his hands and knees on the floor, while another fucked him from behind, and the third got his cock sucked in the front.

Jeremy was fully hard now and I slipped his joggers down to free his cock. It bobbed free, hitting against his stomach and leaving a wet spot on his T-shirt before I took it firmly in hand.

He spread his legs to accommodate me, a breath-less moan escaping him, while his eyes locked on the screen.

The men in the film changed positions. The one on his hands and knees stayed where he was, but the other two switched.

"Jesus. He's sucking him off after he's been fucking him?" It came out on another moan, so it didn't sound as disgusted as it was probably meant.

"Some men like that, you know." I leaned in to press a kiss on the corner of his mouth. "To fuck and then be sucked off afterwards."

"Do you like it?"

"I certainly wouldn't say no if offered." In fact, I found arseplay incredibly hot in and of itself, but I'd always known with Jeremy that it hadn't been in the cards. And I'd been okay with that, because I loved him—but Chad was open to it, seemed to get off on it even, and it was like a dream come true.

"Ah, shit." Jeremy took the laptop and put it down on the sofa, then he straddled my thighs and frantically zipped down my trousers. I lifted my hips as much as I was able with his weight on me, and he pulled both trousers and pants down.

My cock stood proud, waiting for attention, and it got it as Jeremy wrapped his hand around the both of us.

I switched between watching Jeremy and watching the screen, where the lads had switched sides again. The man in the middle was getting right and truly fucked. The last one had come inside him, and the semen trickled down his thighs as the other one thrust his own cock inside.

Seemed the first one had more inside though, because he wanked off into the bottom's mouth.

"Do you wish he was here?" Jeremy must've noticed where my eyes had strayed. He leaned in close, asking the question against my ear. "Do you wish we were three instead of two?"

"I do." I couldn't lie. I wanted Chad to be a proper part of our relationship too. "I don't want any of us to feel left out, *ever*."

Jeremy stopped stroking us, and when he climbed off my lap I was sure I'd managed to hurt him with my admission. But he only got on his knees on the floor and spread my legs further apart so he could fit in-between. He stroked my cock a few times, almost thoughtfully, before glancing up at me.

"Did you fuck him bare?"

"Yeah." I knew were this was headed. Jeremy's dislike of anything anal. "But we showered afterwards."

"Good." And he swallowed me down. For all he didn't care for anal, Jeremy was a bloody expert on oral.

A loud groan escaped me as he deep-throated me and I involuntarily bucked my hips up, which was too much even for him, considering he'd taken all my length in already.

He slapped my thigh playfully as he pulled back. "Haven't you already had sex once today? You shouldn't be so impatient. Slag." It was said as a joke though as he went back down on me.

This time I managed to keep my hips on the sofa. Instead I buried my fingers in his hair, though I made certain it wasn't hard enough to hurt him, just enough to be felt.

He was right though. It wasn't often I had sex every day—Jeremy and I had tapered off from that after the initial so-called honeymoon phase had been over. We'd used to have sex maybe once or twice a week until I'd cheated on him. So having sex for the second time in a day was an oddity, but also a good one. I liked sex, there was no other way around that.

Jeremy could go a long time without sex. He was a lot more patient than I was, as well as he didn't have such a high libido. But when I initiated it, he was always willing to go.

As I'd already come once that day, I could go a bit longer than usual now. Or I tried to anyway, but Jeremy's mouth working me was too good to be able to keep the orgasm in.

Jeremy's mouth left my cock with a loud *pop*.

"Come on me." He stroked me furiously, just like he knew I liked it.

My muscles tightened—and then I did shoot, hitting his cheek, his jaw, and his mouth, as well as some trickling down his fingers.

While I came down from my high, Jeremy licked the semen off his fingers, then used said fingers to wipe it off his face and lick that off too.

I slid further down on the sofa so my arse was at the very edge of it. "Come up here, Jem, and I'll suck you off too."

He didn't have to be asked twice. He climbed up over me again until the tip of his cock nudged against my lips.

I opened up to him and he slid inside, cock already slick from pre-come.

I covered my teeth with my lips, then set to task, trying to suck him as well as he'd done me, though I knew my skills in this department weren't as exquisite as his were.

It didn't take him long to come and I swallowed it all, allowing him to thrust into my mouth to get the last few spurts out.

"Bloody hell." Jeremy collapsed atop me, arms going round my neck and forehead resting against my cheek.

"Yeah." I wrapped both my arms around his back,

holding him in close. Our spent, sticky dicks pressed together, but neither of us could get it up again this quickly.

The porn video on the laptop had stopped playing a long time ago, so the only sounds in the room were our laboured breathing.

"When Chad comes home tomorrow, we should have a chat." Jeremy kissed my cheek sloppily. "Figure out how we want things before we take it any further. There's a lot to figure out."

"Yeah." I stroked my hands lazily up his back. "Yeah, there is. But I think we will. Figure it out, that is."

"I think so too." Another sloppy kiss, this one to the corner of my mouth. "We're all ready to take things further."

Nothing could please me more than to hear that.

CHAPTER 7

*N*ext morning, I found something that worried me to the point our talk had to be postponed.

Chad's prescription bottles were in the cabinet in the bathroom—while Chad himself was at Wynn's place, sans them.

"Shit." *Shit, shit, shit.* I didn't know how long he could go without taking his medicine for them to stop working, for him to relapse, but as he'd just started on them, I imagine it couldn't be long.

Had they even taken proper effect after this short a time?

I headed to work, worrying all the while. I had to teach the first hour, but after that I had two available where I was supposed to do grading. Instead I was online researching Chad's disorder again, like I'd done so often before.

However, now I focused more on the medicine and living a healthy lifestyle than the bipolar disorder itself. It seemed there was lots he could do to keep relapses from happening, besides taking his medicine at the right time every single day.

It also said a bipolar person should *never* stop taking their medicine, as it could have dangerous effects.

"Is he home yet?" I called out the minute I was inside the door.

"No." Jeremy came out from the kitchen, wiping his hands off on a cloth.

"I've been reading up on things." I threw all the printed out pages on the table. "And he should *never* stop taking his medicine without consulting his doctor."

Jeremy frowned. "Has he stopped?"

"His tablets are here—but he's not."

Jeremy's frown cleared as he realised the implications. "I know where Wynn lives. Let's head over there right away—and bring his medicine with us."

Great idea. I got the bottles while Jeremy got dressed, then we headed outside into the chilly spring air.

"I didn't even think about his medicine." Jeremy ran a hand over his face.

"Well, it's new, innit, so it hasn't turned into a habit yet." I'd forgotten all about them too, until I'd seen them in the cabinet.

"This is something we need to have a chat about." Jeremy buried his hands in his pockets now. "Like, are we going to have to watch and make sure he takes his pills? I read up on bipolar too, and many people with the disorder tend to go off their meds. And he's admitted he likes being manic."

"You were right last night. We *do* have a lot to talk about. And hopefully we will, as soon as his friend's feeling better again." I hoped Wynn wasn't feeling so well he started in on the drugs again though—and especially that Chad didn't take any.

Just because he'd been feeling well lately didn't have to mean he didn't miss the drugs and the alcohol, and that would interfere with his medicine. If they even worked. It could just be he was back in a normal mood for the time-being.

It was hard to know. And I'd read a lot about it lately, and about medicine especially today. Effects of medicine, after-affects, statistics on how many went off their medicine and for how many the medicine didn't work. Most interesting had been the part about how many managed to keep their bipolar disorder in check by changing their lifestyle and avoiding their triggers.

"You should read everything I printed out today."

"I have read up on the disorder."

"Yeah, I have too. But everything from today is specifically about medicine and bipolar disorder. Quite interesting reading, but some disturbing and some worrying information." I wondered if Chad would do better in time, or if we would always have to worry about him spiralling back into severe mania or down into heavy depression.

I still wanted to hit myself for not noticing just how bad he'd been back when I'd only been his teacher. But I'd only seen him for a couple of hours a day, so I couldn't have recognised a disorder I'd known nothing about.

But that day I'd slept with him … I should've seen it then. He'd been acting so weird.

Something had been very wrong.

I'D BEEN STANDING with the phone to my ear, ready to dial the emergency number.

"Who you calling?"

"Bloody 999." He wasn't making any sense. He was out of his *mind*.

"You don't have to do that, I'm not sick. I'm perfectly healthy. Look, I'm even hard again!" He threw his arms wide and looked down on himself, where his erection was pressing against his jeans. "You need the A&E, since you can't seem to get it up again. Now *that's* not normal." He twirled around like he was a bloody dancer. "I have to go. Things to do, people to bang, a life to live! You stay here and watch the stars. They're beautiful!"

I'd forgotten all about the phone. "What stars?" What the hell was he on about? There were no stars inside. Not outside either, for that matter, as it was the middle of the *day*.

But he was gone.

And I stood there with the phone like an idiot.

"Chad!" I dropped the phone down and ran after him, but by the time I'd managed to get my own stunned arse out from the lounge and out of the college, Chad was already gone. If we'd lived in a rural town I could've got lucky if I went looking for him, but in the middle of London... there wasn't a chance of finding him.

I slunk back inside, my mind rolling.

The condom we'd used was still on the floor— and it stood out so much my gaze was instantly drawn to it. A flash of guilt stabbed me right through the chest. I hurried to find a wad of paper, then bundled it up in it. I stuffed it into a pocket in my briefcase, because I couldn't let it lay in the trash at my desk. What if someone saw it?

I liked my job, and I preferred to keep it. If it came out I'd fucked a student, the chances of that happening were slim.

Not to mention my relationship... What would Jeremy say to me getting it on with one of my students? For him, I reckoned, it would be more about the sex part than the student part, but still... I might've just screwed everything up.

I wheeled my chair back over to my desk, then sank into it and buried my face in my palms.

What've I done?

My problems weren't forefront right now though. Something was wrong with Chad. I'd seen it all day. He was usually morose and silent, making himself as small and possible. But today... today he'd been vibrating. His newly acquired bruises hadn't even begun to fade, yet he seemed to be the happiest lad on earth.

Not to mention the way he'd jumped me. I'd been too weak to resist someone who I cared about and who so obviously wanted me. And it'd been good, of course it had, even if it'd had been a bit hurried.

Then afterwards... he'd zoned out on me, staring

TANGLED

transfixed at the ceiling, then he'd given me quite a look as he wanked himself off.

And then the I-love-you-s. I hadn't told him that, yet he'd spoken to me as if I had. I didn't love him. I *cared* for him, of course. He'd been a part of my life for the past four months. I'd spent so much more time with him than any of my other students.

But his behaviour today ... It wasn't like I'd ever seen him before. He'd been vibrating with energy, he'd been frantic, he'd apparently heard me say something I *hadn't*, and what stars had he been on about? What stars had he seen?

I let my hands drop down, then I quickly searched up his home number. I didn't think he'd made it there, it hadn't sounded like he'd planned on going home, but his behaviour was troubling and something needed to be done.

"'Lo?" A low, deep, hoarse voice answered the phone.

"Mr. Foster? I'm Dion Stryker, your son's English teacher—"

"The fuck's he done now?" It came out a grunt.

"Eh, nothing. I'm just ringing you because I'm worried—"

"If he's done nothin', then why're you callin'?" His tone of voice got higher. "Leave us the fuck alone!" And with that yelled in my ear, he hung up on me.

I blinked as I listened to the *peeps* signalling I'd lost contact with him. *No help from there then.*

~

I SHOULD'VE DONE something more. Instead I'd gone home and told Jeremy about having cheated on him. I'd been worried though, and I sought Chad out only to tell him we couldn't see each other again—and that I'd chosen Jeremy.

He'd been at college one more day—enough to yell at me—and then he'd quit altogether. It'd been three weeks until I'd seen him again, and that had been when he'd been in hospital with alcohol poisoning.

Jeremy had seen him before me, even. He'd taken him in and cleaned him up and put him to bed in the guest room—which until then had been *his* new room, as he hadn't wanted to share a bed with me after I'd cheated on him.

How different things were now.

Jeremy and I were good again—we were close again—and we were both getting close to Chad as well. I couldn't help but think things could've been different if I'd done something that day though—that Chad wouldn't have had to spiral so far before getting the help he needed.

"What are you feeling guilty about now?" Jeremy's voice broke into my thoughts.

"Nothing."

"Come on." He bumped his shoulder against mine.

I blew out a breath, then told him what I'd been thinking about.

"It's not your fault, Dion. You couldn't know it was as bad as it was."

"But I could've finished that call."

"He ran away. What were they supposed to do? Look all over the city for him?" Jeremy shook his head. "Nothing that happened is your fault. Well, sleeping with him was, I reckon, but not his mental health or his home life or anything else."

I threw him a shrewd glance. "Does it still bother you? That I cheated on you? Even if the three of us are working things out now?"

He was silent a minute as we trudged along. "Well, yeah. Of course it bothers me, but... I know Chad now. I see the appeal. He's sweet and caring underneath his disorder—and even that has its charming sides. When he's manic—without the psychosis and the irritability—he's quite nice to be around. He's excited, can't shut his mouth, jumps from one topic to the next so fast I almost can't keep up. He's got so much *energy*."

"So you like Chad when he's manic?"

Jeremy hit my shoulder. "There are sides to the mania that are good, but it spirals out of control and it does so very quickly. But I like the calm, sweet lad underneath it all too. Him most of all, actually."

I smiled, his words warming me from the inside out. "I do too."

"Since you absolutely had to go fall for someone else, I think you made a great choice. Not a choice that's going to be easy for any of us, but a great choice nonetheless."

No, easy was not a word to put on it. A three-way relationship wouldn't be easy in the first place—but add to that a severe mental illness that would likely never go away, and things were a lot more complicated.

But as long as I'd have the two of them, I'd take complicated any day. The past two years had been strangely uncomplicated—Jeremy and I had clicked immediately, his parents were amazing, and we had our flat and our jobs, even if his wasn't his dream job. We had each other.

Now we had Chad too, added into the dull life we'd led.

And one thing was certain: life wouldn't be dull again.

CHAPTER 8

*C*had seemed calm when he opened the door.

I took him in swiftly, but everything seemed to be okay. He was surprised to see us though, as was evident from the way his eyes widened.

"What're you doing here?"

"Your medicine." I held out the plastic bag. "You forgot it."

"Oh." He stared at said bag as if there was something toxic inside it. "Right." He took it with hesitation and glanced inside.

I took in the shaggy auburn hair and freckles adorning Chad's nose and cheeks. He was so different from Jeremy, with his thick brown hair and smooth face. Chad was small and slight, though much of that was from malnutrition and bad habits, whereas Jeremy was tall and fit and healthy with no bad habits to speak of.

Yet I'd fallen for both of them. It made absolutely no sense, yet it was the absolute truth.

"How's Wynn?" Jeremy asked.

"Bit better. I got him to eat your food last night, and he's taking a shower now." He seemed pleased, which was good. It didn't sound like much, but if Wynn had been depressed to the point of being unable to move... then perhaps it was. He looked back down into the bag. "Guess I have to take these now." He backed off from the door. "Come in."

He headed over to the kitchen, got a glass of water, then took a tablet from each of the bottles.

I watched him until he'd swallowed them both. I couldn't help it—I didn't quite trust him, especially not after the hesitation once I'd handed it to him.

"Do you feel like it's working?"

"Don't know." He dragged a hand through his hair, messing it up further. "I have good days, you know, before I was in hospital and they started giving me all these different drugs. They could last a while too, it's not like it's all rapid cycling all the time." He shuffled back out of the kitchen. "Speaking of which, I've got a therapy session where we'll try and figure out if they *are* working." He froze suddenly, eyes going wide again. "Oh shit! Oh shit *shit shit.*"

"What?" I stared as he dived for his mobile phone, which was on the coffee table.

"I missed it. It was at two."

And now it was over five. It was closed now, anyway. "Go there tomorrow morning and explain. Maybe your psychiatrist will have an appointment available."

He looked dubious. "I guess I can try."

"You have to try." I was worried all over again now. "You just started on these medicines. They might not be right for you or the right dosage, and that's what your psychiatrist and your doctor is there to help you figure out. To help you avoid any damage to your body." I'd read about what could happen if they took too high a dosage of say, anti-psychotics, which he was *on*. It could be toxic for the body.

"Come on, it's not that important." He snorted.

"Yes, it is. Too high a dosage could damage your liver. Too low a dosage won't be of any help at all. You'll relapse."

"How can I relapse if it hasn't even been working?" There was an annoyed tone to his voice now, which worried me, because irritability could be a sign of oncoming mania.

"I'm sorry. Wrong choice of words." It was better to back down. One of the rules of staying stable was no stress. I didn't want to stress him in any kind of way.

"Did you eat some of the food I made?" Jeremy stepped around me to focus on Chad. "I made it for the both of you."

"I did." Chad nodded vigorously. "It was very good."

The irritability had already gone away, which I hoped meant he wasn't on the verge of another manic episode.

Footsteps alerted me to another presence, and I turned to find Wynn standing in his bedroom doorway, dressed in a black T-shirt and black joggers, feet bare and hair dripping water.

"How're you feeling?" Chad rushed past both Jeremy and me, to face his friend. "A shower was good, right?"

Wynn turned cold eyes on him. "You can leave now. And take your boyfriends with you."

Chad stopped short. "Wynn—"

"I don't want visitors!" Wynn turned on his heels and slammed his bedroom door closed.

Chad rubbed a hand over his forehead, tangling his fingers in his hair and pulling slightly.

Jeremy sidled in close to me. "How about we take him out to dinner? Get his mind off of things."

"That's a good idea." I took the bottles from the counter and put them back in the bag. "Want to go out and eat, Chad?" I called over to him.

"Can't afford it," he muttered to the floor.

"Don't worry. It's on us." I took the bag in hand before walking over to him, sliding my free arm around his shoulders.

"I'm not really dressed to go out anywhere." He plucker at his wrinkled jumper.

"We don't have to go out if you don't want to," I said, able to take a hint.

"I can whip us up something at home." Jeremy ambled over, gaze taking Chad in. "We'd be more comfortable there anyway." He glanced up at me and I nodded quickly. *More comfortable to talk.*

"If it's not too much trouble." Chad drew his bottom lip in-between his teeth. "If you don't want to cook, I guess we could find a place that isn't too fancy."

"Let's see if we find a place to eat on the way back," I said. "If we don't, we can all chip in and make something easy at home."

Chad seemed happy with that suggestion, but not so happy to leave Wynn's flat. Wynn had made himself clear though, so Chad got his shoes and jacket on with a defeated sigh.

"Well, at least he's back to being an arsehole," he said as we headed down the stairs. "I guess that's good."

"How did you two meet exactly?" Jeremy leaned forward slightly so he could look at Chad, who was walking on my other side. "You're quite different people."

"How did we meet..." Chad scratched at his head. "When I failed my GSCEs for the first time, I had to retake the entire year, and then I was put in Wynn's class. He was the only one who spoke to me, and since then we've been friends."

"Is he a good friend?" I could hear from the tone in Jeremy's voice that he didn't think so.

I wasn't going to put any judgement on Wynn's capability of being a good friend or not. I'd had him as my student for two whole years, and though he was intelligent, he hadn't been predisposed to actually *show* it.

I'd had the impression that he hadn't really given a shit about college, as long as he passed. In my opinion, he could've passed with top grades if he'd made an effort—but he hadn't, so he'd only got past with mediocre grades.

"Yeah, he is. He's... he cares, even if he doesn't

show it. Even if he doesn't show it in normal, healthy ways. But he lets me stay whenever I need to." Chad chewed on his bottom lip again. "He takes care of the people he loves. When someone hurt Madison, Wynn beat them up. He would've taken on Dad too, if I'd given him the opportunity, but I never did."

I looked at him. Did he regret not giving Wynn that opportunity? His voice was flat, so it was hard to tell.

"He seems... cold."

Chad finally looked at Jeremy, his green eyes intense. "Wynn's got no reason to be a *warm* person. He is what life's made him. If you think my life's shit ... it's nothing to Wynn's. To what it was, anyway. Now he takes care of himself."

A warning bell rang in my head. "Wynn comes from the same situation you do?" I'd never spotted bruises on him, not once in the two years he'd been in my English class. There were a few times he'd sported bloody knuckles, but that had obviously been his own doing. Probably by beating someone up, as Chad had mentioned.

"Worse. Lots worse." Chad turned his head away. "But I can't talk about it. I promised not to ever tell anybody."

"That's okay." Jeremy smiled tightly at him,

TT KOVE

though Chad couldn't see it. "You shouldn't break your friend's trust. I won't ask anymore."

Chad only nodded at that, but he seemed to relax a bit after that.

I caught sight of a sign down the street. "How about Pizza Hut?"

"Hmm?" They both stared at me.

"For food?" I glanced between them. "It's not fancy, no dress-code, and it's just pizza."

"I like Pizza Hut." Chad perked up, finally looking eager for something.

Jeremy must've seen it too. "Then Pizza Hut it is."

We found a table that was slightly secluded, and as no one was sitting at the tables nearby, we got a bit of privacy. We ordered drinks, perused the menu, and once the waiter came back with the drinks we ordered the food.

"So…" Chad took a drink of his Coke, while his gaze flicked between Jeremy and me. "How did *you* meet?"

A laugh escaped Jeremy, while I leaned back in my chair with a smile. "We met when we were both doing something neither of us like—clubbing."

"So you started out as a one-night-stand?" A slight smile adorned his lips too, but for him it was more like we were sharing a joke he didn't get. And he didn't—not yet.

94

"No. Not at all." Jeremy shut down that thought-process quickly. "We met at the bar, where we were both sitting being entirely uncomfortable. I guess we both recognised a kindred spirit." He turned to me with a warm smile.

"I guess we did. We left the club, anyway, headed to a café that was open late, and there we just talked." It was a good memory. The talk had flowed effortlessly—there hadn't been a single uncomfortable silence between us that night.

Chad's eyes narrowed. "You *talked*? *Only* talked?"

"We did." I felt bad for him, for such a young person thinking that everything was about sex. But then it had been for him, since before he'd even been a teenager. It wasn't right—but for some it was the way of life. "We had coffee and tea, and we talked."

"It was nice. Nice to meet someone where it wasn't all about sex." Jeremy put his hand on my arm and squeezed.

Chad's eyes narrowed further. "I don't believe you. No one meets at a club, leave together, and then only goes for a *chat*. That's not right."

"That's how a proper relationship is built."

The contrast between Jeremy and Chad was even greater now. Not just their looks, but their beliefs and values too. Jeremy thought sex only belonged in a long-term intimate relationship—though he had allowed Chad to seduce him, which had been surprising—whereas Chad believed sex was something to be had at any time. And me? Well, I reckoned I hovered somewhere in the middle of their opposite believes.

Chad's gaze, that had clearly said how much he didn't believe us, turned confused. "So you really only talked? For an entire night?"

"For *weeks*," Jeremy said. "We spent time together, figuring each other out. When we decided to try a relationship, that's when we started having sex."

Chad blinked. "And that... worked? What if you weren't compatible in bed? What would you have done then?"

Colour rose in Jeremy's cheeks and he glanced my way. "We worked it out."

I didn't have a single complaint about our two years together. Not one. Well, except maybe for the way I could've ruined those two years, but other than that I was happy. Had been through the entire relationship.

Chad's lips parted to say something, but our waiter arrived with our pizza just then, so he shut himself up. We'd ordered two big ones, with different toppings, so we could eat from whichever one we wanted.

"Did it work for you?" Chad asked eventually, once we'd prepared our food.

"Did what?" I'd already lost track of where we'd left the conversation.

"Talking, getting to know each other, and figuring things out afterwards. Did that really work?" He stared down at the table, face set in a serious expression.

"Well, yeah, it did. Else we wouldn't have been together for two years." I added salad to my plate, as only pizza would be too one-track.

"That's what they said in therapy when I was in hospital too. That communication is the key, that without it, things won't get better."

"It's important to share one's thoughts and feelings and opinions." Jeremy took the salad after me, put some on his plate, then held it out to Chad. "You want some?"

Chad lifted his head to stare at the salad for a moment. "Um, no thanks." He chewed thoughtfully on a piece of pizza. "Maybe it does work, the whole not falling right into bed. I don't know. I've never had a relationship before."

His whole life was tragic—but I hoped that now, away from his abusive dad and with a diagnosis on hand, he'd do a lot better.

Jeremy, who'd been so set on all three of us

talking together, didn't say anything now, and we ate in silence. I didn't want to ask him out loud, so I tried to convey my question with a look, but he only narrowed his eyes at me, not understanding.

So once we'd finished our pizzas and paid for them, we headed home. It wasn't an uncomfortable silence between us, per say, but it wasn't entirely *comfortable* either.

"You expecting visitors?" Chad asked once we'd locked ourselves into our building.

"No." We didn't really know anyone well enough for them to pop in for a visit—which spoke volume of our social life.

But there was a woman standing in front of our door. She turned once she heard Chad speak, and her eyes widened as they fell on me. "Dion?"

First when I heard her voice did I realise who she was. "Sophia?"

It felt like the floor had fallen away under my feet.

CHAPTER 9

*I*t'd been fifteen years since I'd last seen her.

She'd been just a teenager then—and now here she was, a grown woman. Her chin was raised slightly, defiantly, and she had the same dirty-blonde hair I did, only hers was long and thick and curly.

She didn't look at all like the pimply teenager I'd left.

"Sophia," I said again, the shock of her being right there in front of me starting to wear off. Still, why was she here? Why was she seeking me out now?

"Mum's sick and she wants you to come see her before she dies."

There I got the answer to that. "She's *dying*?"

When she'd first said sick, I'd expected something less severe.

"Yes." Sophia nodded matter-of-factly. "Haven't got long left, that's what the doctors say."

I stared at my sister. She was as frank and matter-of-fact as I remembered her—only I'd though back then that her attitude had been because she was a teenager. I'd thought she'd grow out of it. Apparently not.

"Do you want to come in?" I motioned to our door.

She glanced from it to me. "I've told you what I came here to tell you."

I watched her apprehensively. "Are you angry with me?"

"Why would I be?" She seemed to be honestly puzzled.

She puzzled me too, with her behaviour. Though it was exactly the way I remembered it. "Well, because I left you there. With them."

"They never did me anything." She cocked her head to the side, as if she was trying to figure me out —just as I was trying to figure her out. "Do I have reason to be angry with you?"

"I—I don't know."

"You left. I stayed. There's nothing in there to be angry about." She didn't seem quite sure though.

"Please come in, Sophia." I slid past her to unlock and open the door.

She glanced from me to Jeremy and Chad, both of whom were standing in the background uncertainly.

"All of you, come in." I made motions with my hand as if shooing them inside. They trudged in, one after the other.

"I'll make us some tea." Jeremy headed into the kitchen, and after a moment's hesitation, Chad followed him.

Sophia stared after them. "Your flatmates?"

Since Sophia didn't seem to have changed, I saw no reason to lie. "My boyfriends."

"Oh." It was said in a final tone of voice. Not like it was a major surprise or like she disapproved of my life choices. Just simple acceptance of my words.

"You haven't changed at all."

Her nose wrinkled as her gaze cut to me. "It's been fifteen years. I've changed a lot, actually."

"I meant—" I motioned to her as a whole. "You. Your personality. The outside's different, but the inside's the same."

"Oh. Yeah, I suppose."

A calm settled over me. She was fine. As weird as she'd been back then, but she seemed to be perfectly fine. "It's good to see you again."

Her gaze came back to focus on me. "Okay."

I couldn't stop a chuckle. "You *really* haven't changed." Sophia had always been honest to a fault, and not very good at sentiments or feelings in general. She wasn't very good at reading people either.

"I'm going to sit down." And she did, sitting on the smaller sofa with her hands resting in her lap. She took the flat in, but didn't say anything else.

Jeremy and Chad came back out with the tea and poured cups for us. Sophia watched it until Jeremy pushed a cup towards her.

"I don't drink tea."

Jeremy froze. "You don't drink tea?" Being English, that was unusual. But tea had never been a part of our household back then. Alcohol had been the usual liquid of choice, and us kids had to take what we could find. Usually only water.

"No." Matter-of-factly again.

"Do you want something else? Coffee, Coke?"

"Just water." No please afterwards, which the teachers at school had always given her grief for. But this was Sophia—she wasn't predisposed to try and make people like her, to try and please people by being nice. She said exactly what she meant.

She'd had troubles at school all the time—more than me—yet she'd still been Dad's little princess.

"I'll get it." Chad slinked away.

Jeremy finished pouring tea for the rest of us, then sat down close to me.

"Here you go." Chad set a glass of water in front of Sophia, then sat down at the available space next to Jeremy.

Sophia took a sip of the water as she studied the three of us. "What did you want to talk to me about?"

"I haven't seen you in fifteen years—and you just show up out of the blue because Mum is sick."

"She is."

"How'd you find me?" I hadn't contacted any of them in the past fifteen years. I hadn't thought they'd give a shit.

"I've known where you were for years."

"Years?" I blinked at her in shock. "Then why're you only showing up now?"

"Because Mum wants to talk to you before she dies."

Goddammit. I was reminded of just how much she could annoy me too. "What's wrong with her?"

"Cancer. End-stage. It's spread to everything."

I couldn't tell if she was sad about the fact or not. Was she close to Mum? She hadn't been—she hadn't been close to anyone, though she'd always been Dad's favourite. "Why does she want to talk to me now?"

She shrugged. "Didn't ask."

Of course not. I dragged a hand through my hair and over my face. "This is Jeremy and Chad, in case you were wondering." I motioned to each of them in turn, though I was pretty sure she hadn't been wondering.

"Hello." She nodded politely at both of them, but didn't seem inclined to anything else. Like ask questions.

"What about Dad?" It occurred to me so suddenly that she hadn't mentioned that bastard.

"He's dead."

I cast my gaze heavenwards. "When did that happen?"

"Six years ago."

"Right." At least *he* hadn't wanted to talk to me on his deathbed. "How bad is Mum?"

"She's dying."

"Yes, you said so, but how long has she got left?"

"Days, not more than a week."

I drew in a sharp breath. "And why does she suddenly want to see me *now*, right before she's dying? Surely she's known about the cancer for a while."

Sophia stared at me, puzzled. "I don't know what she's thinking."

"Of course you don't." Sophia had never given

thought to what others were thinking. Or she couldn't. I didn't know which.

"So are you going to go back with me now?"

I dragged both hands over my face this time. "I've got a job." I wasn't even sure I wanted to go back to my hometown and deal with the woman who was too spineless to throw her cheating, alcoholic piece of shit husband out on the streets.

"You have a legal entitlement to take unpaid time off to deal with an emergency involving a dependant."

It was my turn to stare at her. That had been delivered in her usual smooth, aloof voice, but said with such ease like it was something she *knew* and had experience in explaining. "What do you work with?"

"I'm a solicitor."

Just as figured. I suppose that would be a good career for her though. She was intelligent, blunt, and didn't care what others thought of her. And she'd always stuck to the good side of the law, which was a good thing for people actually practicing it. And she didn't possess the ability to become emotionally involved with anyone, so I was sure that helped a lot as she could never be jeopardised in that matter.

"That's great," I said. "Do you like it?"

"It's okay."

"Would you rather be doing something else?"

She shook her head. "No."

So she did like her job then, she just still lacked the ability to show any sort of joy for it. If I'd been a teacher when Sophia had been in school, I would've suggested for the parents to have her checked for a developmental or personality disorder, but then again... maybe the teachers had suggested it, but our parents hadn't given a shit about us much, so they'd let it be.

She looked down at her watch. "So are you coming? I have to get back."

I scratched at my neck awkwardly, mind rolling around in circles. "Are you busy?"

"Yes. I have work in the morning."

"So do I."

"You can call in. Mum is dying and she wants to talk to you before she does." Sophia stood and brushed off her jacket and trousers. She was dressed rather nice, so I suppose her job must be paying her well.

Well, okay, it wasn't like I had the best paying job, but it still required me to dress up, so I suppose I couldn't make that kind of assumption by her clothes. She wouldn't like it if I'd said it out loud, if she was still exactly alike the teenager I remembered.

"Can you give me a moment to think about it?"

She stopped short in her brushing down, glancing again at her watch. "An hour. That's all. I'll head around the corner until then. I saw a small Café there when I parked my car."

"You're welcome to stay here." Jeremy jumped up. "Honestly. I can make you some food, if you're hungry."

"I'd rather go to the Café." Sophia nodded curtly, then swiftly left the flat.

Silence fell over us, while I continued to watch the now closed door.

"So… your sister." Jeremy's voice brought my focus over to him. "She was… not at all like you." He was struggling for words, and it was kind of adorable, actually.

"No, she's…" But then I was struggling just as much to describe her. "She's pretty special. Always was—and it seems she hasn't changed much."

"Are you going to go with her?" Chad leaned forward so he could look directly at me.

I swallowed around the lump stuck in my throat. "I am curious as to what she has to say. And she's my mum… I know she made bad choices for herself and for us all our lives, but she's still the woman who gave birth to me."

If she wanted forgiveness, I wasn't sure I could ever give her that, because I had too many bitter feelings about it all. But I could go and hear what she had to say, listen to her in her last few days.

"I think you should go." Jeremy put a hand on my arm. "She obviously wants to see you."

"Yeah, now she's almost dead." I held back a bitter laugh. "Bit too late to make amends now."

"Maybe she just wants to see you again before she's gone?" Jeremy squeezed. "Lots of people realise the wrong they've done only when they're on their deathbeds."

"But that's a little too late to realise it, and certainly to apologise for it." I'd put everything behind me in the past fifteen years. Of course, I'd spared thoughts for Sophia, but I'd never doubted she'd be able to care for herself. But my parents... I'd put them behind me. It did no good dwelling on that past.

"If I could've seen my mum again, I would've taken the opportunity," Chad said.

But you loved your mum—and she loved you.

I smiled sadly at him. I couldn't in right conscience say I loved mine, because she'd obviously not loved me enough to make sure I had a nice, good, stable upbringing without a whoring, alcoholic dad.

I didn't think that had been too much to expect.

A mother was supposed to love her children, and

want the best for them. And the best was definitely not to be beaten around. Not for her or her kids.

Then again, whatever it was she wanted to talk to me about… if I didn't go now, I would never know. And I wasn't sure I would be okay with that either.

"I think I have to go. I have to know what it is she wants." It didn't have to be anything life-changing, which was my expectation—but on the other hand it could be, and it would be a shame not to hear it. To pay my last respects, even if I didn't hold much respect for her as a person.

"Whatever you decide." Jeremy rubbed my arm now instead of squeezing it, like I needed comfort.

"I'm not upset," I said. "I haven't seen her in fifteen years, and when I left there were only bad blood between us. I'm just curious."

It felt strangely freeing to know that Dad was dead, that I wouldn't suddenly stand face to face with him. With him gone, I could go back there and face Mum. If he'd still been alive… then I wouldn't have wanted to set foot back in my hometown. The place where no one had done anything, even if they must've known what had been going on.

"I guess I have to go pack." Sophia was waiting for me, and it didn't seem like she'd like to be kept waiting for long.

So I packed a small bag with a couple changes of

clothes, then stood in front of Jeremy and Chad in the hallway.

They were both looking at me, and now I wasn't quite sure what to do. I wanted to kiss them both goodbye, but would they be okay with me kissing one in front of the other?

Jeremy cast Chad a sheepish glance, then he stepped forward and kissed me himself. "Safe trip. And ring us, okay? When you get there, and if you need to chat. Doesn't matter what time it is."

"I will." I focused on Chad, who'd bowed his head. I couldn't leave without kissing him too, I couldn't get myself to do it. He deserved it just as much as Jeremy. "Bye. See you soon. I hope I won't be gone for more than a couple of days." I tilted his chin up and pressed a soft kiss to his closed lips.

He blinked at me when I stepped back, and I smiled at him and Jeremy—my two boyfriends— then left to find my sister.

It was time to face my past. No matter what it would bring.

CHAPTER 10

*M*um was clearly dying.

She was lying listlessly in a hospital bed, looking pale and frail and all too small for the bed. Her hair was grey and thinning, her face wrinkled, but still recognisable as the person I'd left behind when I'd run away at sixteen.

Machines were gathered around her, but I had no idea what exactly they were monitoring.

"Hey, Mum." I stepped into her line of sight, face set in a neutral expression. It was weird to see her like that, but it wasn't like I'd never seen her weak before.

There'd been many times I'd tried to help her after she'd taken a beating from Dad, only to be pushed away in anger. When I'd taken a beating, she hadn't even attempted to help me, so eventually I'd given up.

"Dion." Her gaze, tired and shrouded, fell on me. "You came." She tried to push herself further up on the bed, but she was too weak to manage it. Her chest wheezed as she tried to take in a deep breath.

I helped her sit up, fluffing the pillows behind her back. Then I took a seat at the empty chair next to the bed, the one I reckoned Sophia used to sit in whenever she was around.

"Sophia said you wanted to talk to me."

I hadn't been able to stop by the hospital the night before, as the visiting hours had been over, so I'd stayed the night at Sophia's flat. The drive up with her had been uncomfortable, at best. She wasn't one for small-talk, so it had mostly consisted of us both being silent.

"See you," she whispered. "Wanted to see you." Her chest wheezed again, telling me she had trouble breathing all the time, not just while exerting herself.

"Why?" Fifteen bloody years. I hadn't given much thought to my family in at least ten of those, probably more. I really *had* put it all behind me—besides the niggling worry about Sophia. "Sophia said she's known where I was for years. You could've rung before if it was so important."

"I wasn't dying before." Her chest rose and fell,

the wheezing sound still loud after she spoke, like she wasn't getting enough air into her lungs.

"So you only want to see me now because you're dying?" My chest squeezed.

"Yes."

Flat out admitting it. "What's with that? You're breaking me up from my life, from my job, just to satisfy a dying wish? That's selfish." I shouldn't be surprised. She'd been selfish all my life.

"I haven't seen you in so long. One day you were there, the next you weren't."

Bitterness welled up. "How long did it take you to figure out I was gone? You'd been cooped up in bed for weeks by the time I'd had enough."

She turned her head the other way, which was answer enough.

"You've seen me." I pushed myself to my feet. "If you haven't got anything to say to me, I'll be going."

Only thing I heard was her wheezing breath—and that, too, was answer enough.

I left the room without looking back. I'd felt all right going in, but now I felt shitty. Like I'd used to feel fifteen years ago—unloved, uncared for, like I mattered nothing.

I never had mattered—not to them. And I had made peace with that, I truly had. But seeing her again, hearing her words, made it all come crashing back once again.

And it was not a good feeling.

~

I PLANNED to leave for home the minute Sophia got back from work, but she had other plans.

"We have to go to the house. You left a lot of stuff —and you have to sort it out. I'm going to sell it."

And so I sat in the driver's seat, longing to go back to London and my flat and my lads, but instead I was faced with my childhood home. It looked even worse for wear than I could remember it, but then no one had ever bothered to look after the house.

All the money back then had gone to alcohol and the cheapest food at the shop—or take-away, since cooking had always been a bother for Mum.

"If there's something you don't want, it'll be thrown away." Sophia unlocked the front door, the same door I'd once had my head smashed against so I'd lost consciousness.

"I can't imagine I'd want anything."

"Why not?"

"I've managed fifteen years without it, so I think it's safe to say there's nothing I actually need here."

"You can have a look anyway." She led the way

inside.

I hadn't expected my room to still be the way I'd left it, but when she led me up to the loft and I saw everything I'd owned packed into cardboard boxes... I just felt empty.

I didn't even want to look through them. The simple thought of it made me feel ill.

"I am not comfortable with this."

"Why not?" She was honestly puzzled. She just didn't *get* it.

"There's nothing for me here."

She motioned to the boxes. "There's lots of yours here. All of these boxes here, are yours. They have your name on them."

"I can see that." My name, scrawled carelessly in front. My old belongings were probably thrown in the boxes just as carelessly. "I'm going home. There's nothing here."

"You don't need to see Mum again?"

Definitely not. "No. I'm done."

"There'll be a funeral." She stood with her arms crossed behind her back, looking calm and collected as if she wasn't talking about her own Mum's funeral. She seemed closer to her than I did, anyway, what with still hanging around and all.

"When?" Stupid question, but it slipped out.

"That depends on when she dies." This too was

delivered in utter calm, as if it was a simple fact that shouldn't cause any sort of emotion.

Obviously.

I turned away from the boxes, leaving them behind. "You want to go out and eat before I catch the train home?"

"I can drive you back."

"No, you don't have to do that." I'd rather sit on the train than another uncomfortable, silent drive with her. "I'm perfectly capable of taking the train."

"I wasn't saying you weren't." She hurried after me as I left the loft.

I took a quick look around the rest of the house—to torture myself really—but that had changed considerably. The rooms and placement of them were the same, of course, but the interior had been changed completely.

Still, that didn't stop me from seeing and remembering all the places where something bad had happened. The door, where Dad had smashed my head, was only the first one. I'd been knocked over the sofa, against the dining room table, shoved off probably every chair that had existed in the house.

I knew exactly what Chad had been going through with his dad—because I'd gone through the same with mine. Only I'd had other family around, who'd seen it and who hadn't done anything.

I'd had teachers too who hadn't seen it—or who had ignored it—and that was why *I* should've seen what Chad had been going through. More than anyone else, I should've *seen* it.

It killed me that I hadn't, until it had almost been too late. And then the man himself had been dead anyway, so Chad would've been free of his abuse no matter what.

"So, dinner?" I turned to face her only when we were back outside the house.

Sophia's eyes flickered a bit, like they usually had done when she'd been thinking hard. "We could do that, yes."

"And then after, I'll head to the train station."

"I'll ring you when she dies. When I know when the funeral will be. You'll come up here?"

It would take time to get used to her bluntness again. That is, if I would even see her again. "Yes, I—I'll come to the funeral." Maybe Jeremy and Chad could get the day off, so I could show them around my hometown. Show them all the dirt from my past, which I'd never told either of them much about. Not even Jeremy, whom I'd been with for over two years, knew much of what had been going on, though he knew my dad had been abusive.

"I don't want you to be a stranger." She'd been young back then. She couldn't be blamed for not helping me. She'd been just a kid. The people who could be blamed… One was dead and the other about to be.

"I'm not." She was puzzled again. "I'm your sister."

I sighed. "Yes, you are. But we haven't spoken in fifteen years, so we could just as easily be strangers. I want us to keep in touch."

"Oh." She nodded curtly, understanding my meaning. "Okay."

"So…" I scuffled the toe of my foot against the gravel in the driveway. "How about that dinner?"

"Yes. I'm hungry."

"Good." She brushed past me to get into the driver's seat, looking at me expectantly once she was inside and I still hadn't moved.

I turned back to my childhood home, taking it in one last time. No good memories as far as I could remember. It was good that Sophia was going to sell it—maybe it would see some happiness and joy inside it for once.

"Dion? Are you coming?" Sophia had rolled down her window, watching me curiously.

"Yeah." Another lingering look at the house. "Yeah, I'm coming."

Time to put in behind me once and for all.

All of it.

~

IT WAS LATE by the time I came home, and all I could hear as I entered the flat was noises from the kitchen.

"Hello? Jem?" I dropped my bag next to the sofa and headed into the kitchen, where I wasn't met with Jeremy—but with Chad.

"Oh! Hey." Chad whirled around, looking stressed and haggard.

"What are you doing?" I eyed the mess on the counter.

"Trying to cook." He scratched his neck with a grimace. "I'm not very good at it. I've never really cooked anything besides pasta or finished meals."

"Why are you cooking? You hungry?"

"Jeremy's always cooking, so I thought I could try it tonight. Have something for him once he's off from work for once."

"That's very kind of you." I wrapped an arm around his shoulders and drew him in close. "Not very successful, but it's the thought that counts."

Chad leaned into me.

"How are you feeling?" I slid my other hand up his arm, feeling the soft skin on his neck, then tangled my fingers in his shaggy hair. "Medicine working?"

"I think so. So far. I'm feeling... I don't know.

Calm, maybe. Not particularly happy, but not sad either." He hugged me close, head resting against my shoulder. "How're you doing?"

I heard the front door open and close, and then Jeremy stuck his head around the door. He smiled when he saw me, and I held my other arm out for him. He came in for a hug too, and Chad tried to move away, but I kept him exactly where he was.

This was what it was supposed to be like. All three of us, close and together.

"Why are you home already?" Jeremy's hand slid around my back, bumping against Chad's, then settling down next to it over my spine. "I thought you'd be gone at least a couple of days."

"There was nothing for me there." There really wasn't. "Everything I need is right here."

As they both leaned back to look at me, I cupped my palms around each of their necks, and drew them both in for a three way kiss. *Oh yeah.*

This was what I wanted.

Nothing in my hometown made me feel like these two men did. While everything back there just made me feel empty, these two made me feel *alive*.

"I think it's time we have ourselves a chat now."

It was time to finally get this relationship on the right track.

PART III
CHAD

CHAPTER 11

THE NIGHT BEFORE

*O*nce Dion left, a heavy, awkward, and altogether uncomfortable silence settled over Jeremy and I.

I still sat on my side of the sofa, while Jeremy had moved over to take Dion's place from earlier. Which left the entire middle seat between us.

"Do you know much about Dion's family?" I asked, just to have *something* to talk about.

"Not really. He's never liked to talk about that."

I could get why. It wasn't a fun subject to revisit. It was bad enough living through abuse, but to then have to talk about it… I had to, in therapy, but otherwise I would prefer not to. Dad was dead now, anyway, so it wasn't like he could come back and hurt me anymore.

"Would you like to watch a film? It's getting late, but not so late it's time for bed just yet."

"Yeah, that would be nice." Watch a film, on opposite sides of the sofa. Wasn't that a perfectly good opportunity to cuddle? Maybe Jeremy didn't like to cuddle. Maybe he liked to cuddle Dion, but not me, no matter what our kiss had felt like.

Jeremy stood up and went over to the shelf next to the television to browse through their DVDs. "Anything in particular you want to watch?"

"No, that's okay. Whatever you want to watch." I never watched films—never had any at home and could never afford to either buy one or go see them in the cinema. So when it came to films, I was wistfully unaware of what was good and what was not.

Jeremy took out three films, read the back of them, and put two back. Then he headed for the bedroom instead of staying in front of the telly in the living room.

"We've got the DVD player in here." He turned to me before opening the door, motioning with his head.

"Oh." My gaze flicked to the telly, and he was right—I couldn't see a DVD player on the shelf underneath it. "We're going to watch it in there?" *In their bed.*

"You mind?" He was hesitant now, which I definitely didn't want him to be.

"No, not at all." I stood, brushed my joggers down, then followed him in.

Their bedroom was sparsely furnished, with a wide bed, a built-in closet, a dresser—and the DVD player and the telly, on the opposite wall from the edge of the bed.

The sheets weren't made, so the bed looked rumpled. Maybe they'd done more than sleep in it before they'd got up.

Jeremy turned the telly on, put the film in, then stood in front of it waiting for it to load properly.

I didn't know what to do with myself. Which side was I supposed to lie on? Which side was Jeremy's? Did that mean that I was going to be using Dion's side now?

"Ready?" Jeremy slid into the opposite side of where I was standing with a smile directed at me. He still had the remote in one hand, pointed at the player.

"Y-yeah." I sat down tentatively on the bed, then when he didn't say anything, I scooted further in and crossed my legs in front of me. I pushed the thick pillow up so I could lean back against it, and I was actually feeling rather comfortable now.

Jeremy lay stretched out, not bothering to sit up as he clicked play on the menu. The remote was discarded to the bedside table as the film started playing.

"Have you seen this one before?" I didn't bother asking what the name was, because I wouldn't know it anyway.

"Yeah, it's a classic. One of those you can watch more than one time without getting bored, you know?"

I didn't know, but I nodded anyway.

It was hard to concentrate of the film with Jeremy stretched out right beside me. He was in a T-shirt and baggy joggers, like I was, but his clothes showed off all the right places on his body. His biceps, his chest and flat stomach, as well as a bulge in his crotch. It hadn't been noticeable when he'd been standing, but now he was lying down, I could see it clearly outlined.

And it was *hot*. I wanted to thrust my hand down his waistband and rub that bulge until it hardened right up. Maybe just suck it so it hardened inside my mouth. Now that was a thought.

I uncrossed my legs and put the one closest to him up, so he couldn't get an accidental look at my crotch. But when I glanced down, nothing had happened there. I was still *soft*, even if the kind of thoughts I'd just had would've hardened me right up, I was all *flaccid*.

What the hell?

That just wasn't right. I desired Jeremy, and the fact I still hadn't truly been with him made my fantasies all the more erotic. I had wanked him off, right smack in the middle of mania, but I couldn't remember how he'd looked or how it'd felt or how big he'd been. Everything from that encounter was a blur.

"You know I like you, right?" I had to say something. Though I had initiated that kiss, so he should know it already. Still, it was out there now.

He looked at me, eyes dark and unreadable. "I know, but we decided to take it slow, didn't we?"

"Yeah." I bit down on my lower lip. "I'm not very good at taking things slow. I've never done that before. But then I've never had a relationship before either."

"By taking things slow, we make sure this is something we really want." His gaze searched mine. "We make sure it's *right*."

"I already feel it's right. It's right with Dion—and with you too."

He continued to watch me searchingly. "From a kiss?"

"And from spending time with you." I wrung my

hands together. "I like spending time with you. You're caring and you're kind, and you'll do anything you can for Dion—and me too. I mean, you even go check up on Wynn if I ask, and *no one* really likes him."

"You like him. That's good enough."

The film we were supposed to be watching was forgotten as I curled up on my side so I could face him properly. "No one's ever done anything for me before. But I really appreciate all you've done. You even helped me once you found out who I was, before you knew me, and you could've kicked me out, but you didn't."

"I wasn't happy once I found out who you were, but I could've never kicked you out." If I read his face correctly, he was telling the absolute truth. "Besides, it was Dion I was unhappy with, not you. He's the one who was in a relationship. But I've already told you all this."

"Yeah, you have." I bowed my head. "I keep bringing up the same things over and over again. It must be annoying."

"Not really." He put a hand on my knee, squeezing. "And like I've mentioned, communication is important. If you need to talk it over again and again, then that's what we'll do."

I slid down on the bed a bit, until my head

rested against the pillow. "How long did it take from you met Dion till you had sex?" I couldn't get over the fact that they hadn't had sex right away. I'd always had sex with people I fancied, and though it had never turned into anything more, the sex had been good and memorable. In some cases, anyway.

Jeremy's expression turned thoughtful. "Weeks. Maybe even a month."

I was flabbergasted. "How could you keep your hands off each other?"

"It's easy if you're determined to." He grinned. "Well, okay, it wasn't *easy*. We're blokes, we like sex —but building a strong foundation was more important."

I knew Dion was a decade older than me, but I had no idea about Jeremy. "How old are you?"

"I'll be twenty-eight this year."

I did a quick count in my head. "And you were all calm and collected and wanted to build a foundation with someone when you were, what, twenty-three, twenty-four?"

His grin morphed into a soft smile. "I've never been the type of bloke to shag around. I've always wanted a relationship, someone to be with in every sense of the word. Like my parents. They've been happily married all my life."

I tucked my arm under my cheek. "And that's what you want too? Something to last a lifetime?"

"Yeah." He nodded, all kinds of certain.

I only grew more weary though. "And you see it with Dion?"

"I knew there was something special there when we met. When we spent that whole night just talking, and the next time we met, we hung out. It was nice to meet a bloke who wasn't just interested in sticking his dick places, you know."

"I don't know. All people have ever wanted with me was to stick their dicks inside me."

Jeremy blinked, startled, and his focus was completely on me again. "It's not like that anymore."

"I've already had sex with both you and Dion. I was manic the first time with you both, but it doesn't change the fact that we *have* had sex."

Jeremy rolled onto his side. "You know what Dion was watching on the laptop the other day?"

"No?" Should I know?

Jeremy grinned wickedly. "Porn. Three-way porn. For research."

Now that was promising. "Really?"

"Yeah. It was…" He struggled for the words, but the smile on his face told me everything.

"You got it on, huh?" I felt a stab at that, but of course they'd get it on if they were both up for it.

They were together, after all. I wanted that too, to just be able to be with my bloke—*blokes*—whenever I wanted to be.

He must've seen something on my face. "Does it bother you?"

"A bit, yeah. I want that too. To be comfortable with you, to watch porn with you, to have an impromptu shag whenever we please."

He leaned over, hand stroking my cheek. "We'll get there."

"Maybe we already are there?"

He stared at me. "Maybe." Then he bent his head and kissed me, and I almost stopped breathing altogether.

Not for long though, as I started answering the kiss, letting my lips move against his. I parted them, pressed my tongue against his, and when he let me in I took proper advantage of it.

I arched up against him and he wrapped his arms around me, pulling us close together. He smelled faintly of aftershave and there was a hint of stubble on his jaw and lower cheeks, which rasped against my own smooth skin that never seemed to grow a beard.

I was so close I could feel him harden against me, but I... I didn't.

Nothing happened down there—nothing at all,

and it was frustrating and embarrassing and *humiliating*.

What if he thought I didn't really fancy him anyway? Maybe he thought I was just with him so I could be with Dion? And it wasn't like that. I wanted Jeremy, I *did*.

Except my body was a traitorous sack of shit that didn't even want to get aroused when I had a handsome, kind, willing man pressed against me.

Jeremy pulled away, eyes searching mine. "You okay?"

"Y-yeah." *No.* "That was really good. I guess I'm just... tired." The lamest excuse ever. But what else was I supposed to say? That I suddenly couldn't get it up? Now that would be the embarrassment of the century.

He pressed another close-mouthed kiss to my lips. "How about we just watch the film, huh? Or you can sleep, if you're tired. I don't mind."

I did. While he focused back on the film, which he'd lost the entire beginning of, I dosed off—and soon fell asleep altogether. The last thing I remembered was him tucking the duvet around me.

CHAPTER 12

I was nineteen years old.

This meant I constantly sported boners, with or without the rest of me's approval. I woke up with morning wood *every single day*, but today… I did not.

I stumbled into the bathroom, relieved myself, then took a good, long look at myself in the mirror. I looked good, for once. No bruises, well rested, well fed. There was nothing wrong with me.

Except there was.

I opened the cabinet and grabbed the two bottles of medicine. One antipsychotic and one mood stabiliser.

Antipsychotic.

A side effect of that one was decreased sexual desire—and even sexual dysfunction.

"Bloody hell no." Sex was all I knew, all I was good at. I wasn't going to let my whole damn sex drive go away. What was I going to do without it? I was getting into a relationship with not one, but two blokes, and that required sex. Sex was good!

I sat the bottles on the counter and rubbed at my temples. A headache was forming. I was freaking out.

"No, this isn't happening. I can't let this happen." I snagged the antipsychotic, strode out of the bathroom and into the toilet, then opened it and emptied the entire contents into the toilet, which I flushed the minute all the tablets had landed in the water.

I watch the water swirl—the tablets with it—then drain out before being filled again with clear water, devoid of any antipsychotic.

"Fuck that shit." But I put the bottle back in the cabinet, because I was pretty sure Jeremy would react if he saw it wasn't there. Dion sure would, and though he wasn't here right now, he'd be home soon and he'd notice instantly.

I did take the mood stabiliser—after praying to no one in particular that it didn't have the same side effects. I didn't think it had. The doctor had explained it to me, but I hadn't paid much attention.

I did remember his comment about sexual dysfunction though, and just *no. No, no, no.*

If I ever had an experience like last night again, I might just die of humiliation. What nineteen year old couldn't get it up, anyway?

It'll come up now. And then we can finally shag—all three of us, when Dion comes home.

Jeremy came rushing out of the bedroom when I finished in the bathroom.

"I'm late! I'm working double shifts today, and I'm late for my early shift at the Café!" The bathroom door slammed closed after him.

I stood in the same place I'd stopped, but now I forced myself into the kitchen. Food. I needed food. Apparently a healthy diet was one of the key elements to manage my mental illness, and now I'd flushed one pair of medicine down the toilet, I should try to stick to the things I could control.

When Jeremy came rushing *out* of the bathroom, I was nibbling on a piece of bread.

"See you tonight, okay?" he called as he hurried past the kitchen door.

"Yeah. I'm not going anywhere." Not tonight, anyway, though I *had* plans for the day. See my therapist, go see Wynn. Lots to do.

He was out the door in a flash, leaving me all on my own, still nibbling on the bread. It didn't taste very good, not even with jam on it, and I was tempted to just throw it away. Still, I wanted to *try* to do good—and hopefully it would turn out to be good *for* me.

It must be. Surely something had to help?

Besides medicine that took away your entire sex drive, that was.

I KNOCKED TENTATIVELY on Wynn's door, unsure what kind of mood he was in today. When he'd thrown me out—and Dion and Jeremy with me—he'd been in a foul one, but I was on my own today so maybe he'd be more lenient.

"Of course it's you." He didn't look at all happy to see me, but he left the door open as he strode back into his flat, so I suppose I must be welcome anyway.

"How are you feeling?"

"How am I supposed to be feeling?" So Wynn was in a snappy, sulky mood. I figured he was allowed to be, after everything that had happened.

I sunk down next to him on the sofa. "I flushed all my antipsychotic tablets down the loo."

He froze, then slowly turned his head towards me. "Now why would you do that?"

"It has unwanted side-effects."

"All medicine has side-effects. Whatever the fuck it is, nausea, bloody diarrhoea, isn't it worth it to keep yourself grounded? To keep yourself from jumping off my fucking balcony because you think you can fly?" He pointed at said door to make his point, then he grabbed me by the front of my jumper and jerked me in close. "I'm not losing you too, you hear me?"

"You're not going to." My voice shook. "You're not."

"If you're not on antipsychotic—"

"I'm on the mood stabilisers!"

His eyes narrowed. "Are those going to stop you from going mental?"

I didn't know, so I didn't answer him. Instead I just stared into his dark eyes, which were still narrowed and angry.

"I thought not." He pushed me away so roughly and quickly I fell back on the sofa, hitting my head on the armrest.

"Ow," I muttered, feeling it with searching fingers.

"Go to your fucking doctor and get a new prescription." Wynn crossed his arms over his chest. "Fucking do it, Chad, so you won't go mental again."

"I've got an appointment with my psychiatrist later." I wasn't sure I was going to say anything about the tablets though. I didn't want to go back on them if it meant I couldn't have sex—or even get turned on. It wasn't worth it. I had the most amazing sex when I was manic, after all. "All the times we had sex… did I ever have trouble getting it up?"

Wynn grimaced. "More like have trouble getting it *down*. You have any idea how long I've had to fuck you sometimes for you to come? Bloody exhausting is what it is. I've never met anyone with the amount of stamina you have."

I chewed nervously on my bottom lip. "Have I always been manic during those times?"

"How the fuck should I know? I always thought you were on drugs." He turned away so I couldn't see his face anymore, which was a tell-tale sign that he was getting emotional. "I couldn't know you were bipolar."

"Of course not. No one knew that." I scooted in closer to him and put my hands on his back, fanning them out. I was afraid he'd push me away again, but he didn't.

He must be really upset if he allowed me this close.

Putting my forehead down against one of his shoulder blades, I took a deep breath. "Could've been the drugs, you know that. Same symptoms, with the hallucinations and all that. But drugs only made the mania worse, or so they say. I always felt great, but no one else agrees."

He didn't say anything. I knew he was listening though, because he was tense.

"They want to give me medicine that lowers sexual function. I'm nineteen years old, and they're giving me drugs that can cause erectile dysfunction. If I can't have sex, what can I do then?"

"I don't know," he mumbled.

I slid my arms around his chest, hugging him fully now. "I'm so sorry I couldn't go to the funeral. I was going to—but they sectioned me. I'm so sorry."

A beat of silence, then, "Do you want to go with me to his grave?"

Of course I wanted that. I couldn't say no—not when he'd asked me in that low, broken voice. Wynn was even more broken than I was, and we only had each other now.

Well, I had someone else too, but he only had me.

And if he wanted me to go with him, then that's what I would do.

ONLY A WHITE CROSS with a scribbled name told us it was Madison's grave.

Wynn stood stony-faced at my side. "She can't even get him a proper headstone."

"I think they have to wait for that until the grave sinks?" I wasn't sure, but something teased at my memory. "I think it was like that with my mum. Like, they can't place the real gravestone until the ground's smooth or something."

Now there was a massive pile of dirt signalling where the coffin had been buried.

"Maybe." Wynn frowned. "I'll have to check it out. If she won't get him a proper headstone, I will."

"Those are expensive. Can you afford that?" He worked as a bartender, but his drug dealing gig paid a lot more.

"I'll have to find a way. He *deserves* a proper stone."

Yeah, he did. Madison had been the most important person in Wynn's life. Dad, on the hand, he *didn't* deserve it. His grave would be just as fresh as Madison's were, which meant he'd have one of the tree crosses as well. I hoped Harriet hadn't planned on spending her money on one of those stones— because if she had, she could just forget about it.

"Do you think it was my fault?" Wynn's voice broke over the last two words.

"Of course not. Madison wanted to die—nothing was going to stop him."

A convulsion seemed to go through Wynn, and then he crouched down and touched the moist dirt. He drew in a shaky breath, then bowed his head.

I watched him grieve in silence for his boyfriend, feeling something heavy settle in my stomach. Wynn had no one—while I had more people in my life than I'd ever had before. I had two potential boyfriends. I had my aunt—and I had Wynn. And Wynn had no one but me, who couldn't be trusted for a second.

Maybe I should get a new prescription. Maybe I could mention it to my psychiatrist, so she could change the dosage. Maybe it would help.

"I will do it."

"Do what?" His voice was hoarse—another sure-tell sign that he was upset. Was he crying?

"I will get a new prescription. A new dosage."

He drew in another shaky breath. "Go do it now."

"What about you?" I didn't want to leave him in the cemetery alone, not when he was crying in front of Madison's grave.

On the other hand, maybe he'd let it all out if I left —and feel better afterwards. Wasn't that a saying, that you felt better after crying? Because it released the happy-hormone or something?

"I'm fine. *Go.*" He waved a hand at me without so much as turning around. "You need your medicine."

I licked my dry lips, still not quite sure if I should leave him alone or not. "Can I come by tomorrow?"

He only nodded, but it was promise enough. I'd come by—and he'd let me in.

～

My psychiatrist was *not* happy with me flushing the old prescription down the toilet—but she adjusted the dosage some and wrote out a new one. I weighted it in my hand as I stood in front of the mirror.

She'd told me to take the new one *right away*, but I couldn't get myself to do it. I had it, anyway, so if things got out of control, I could take a tablet then.

I put it in the cabinet next to the mood stabilisers, then threw away the old bottle. It wasn't like I needed that one to hold up appearances anymore.

Speaking of appearances... It was late now, so it wouldn't be long until Jeremy came home from his double shifts. He'd be hungry—and I had the brilliant idea of trying to cook something good for him.

After all, a way to a man's heart was through his stomach right?

CHAPTER 13

"I think it's time we have ourselves a chat now."

The words travelled like fire through me, exciting me and scaring me at the same time. A chat could be a good thing—or it could be a really bad thing.

But the three-way kiss Dion had just pulled us into foretold something good to come, so I willingly let myself be steered out of the kitchen and onto the sofa.

"What happened to the kitchen?" Jeremy asked once he was sitting. He'd willingly let himself be steered as well.

I grimaced. "I tried to cook. It didn't go so well."

He chuckled. "What did you do, murder something in there?"

"Might as well have."

Dion pushed the coffee table out of the way, then sat down on the floor. "Lets sit here so we can all face each other."

I pushed myself off the edge, my arse making a bit of a harder meeting with the floor than necessary, but not so bad I couldn't continue to sit there.

We sat in somewhat of a semi-circle—or a triangle maybe, as we were three. *Triangle. Threesome. Triad.* All words that could be used for us. Hopefully, anyway.

"What did you want to talk about?" I bunched the hem of my jumper in my palms, hiding my hands from view, and hunched my shoulders nervously as I glanced between them.

"Everything." Dion looked at Jeremy. "You said you wanted to talk. And you're right. We should get everything out in the open. Resolve all of this."

I didn't say anything, didn't know what. They both had been planning this talk? Everything could mean a lot. What *exactly* was it they wanted to talk about?

Jeremy cleared his throat and I could tell he was nervous too. "Dion and I have been together two years. We know each other's habits and quirks, and we're used to living together. Having a third person around all of a sudden, is a new adjustment."

I still didn't say anything. He hadn't asked a question, after all.

"I want to start with Jeremy." Dion gave me a look, it could be all from supporting to apologetic, I couldn't tell. "I'm the one who cheated and brought Chad into our lives. How do you feel about that?"

My eyebrows rose. Was this going to be like a bloody therapy session, where we asked all the question and answered them truthfully?

"I didn't like it at first, I have to admit that. I was angry with you, bitter about you cheating on me after so long. But..." He cast me a smile that was *definitely* apologetic. "I felt sorry for Chad. He'd been given a shitty hand in life, and the more time I spent with you, the more I grew to like you."

Butterflies were going wild in my stomach now.

"Do you have any doubts, Jem? You suggested a three-way relationship in the first place, but it has never been what you wanted."

Oh God.

I was sitting there with my heart in my throat now. What if he did have doubts? Though, if he'd had, he wouldn't have kissed me like he had last night.

Jeremy let out a breath, then smiled. "I'm just getting surer and surer every day." He leant over to put a hand on my knee. "I like you a lot, like I told you last night. Last night was so good, just spending time together in bed like that, talking, getting everything out there... Yeah, Dion, I'm sure."

Dion regarded us curiously. "What did you two do last night?"

"Watched a film. Talked, kissed." Jeremy tilted his head slightly. "It was good, right?" A bit of hesitation in his voice now.

"Yes!" Of course it was. How couldn't it have been?

Jeremy pulled back now, and looked at Dion, who was watching me thoughtfully. "How do you feel about entering into our already established relationship?"

I jerked in surprise at finally being asked a question, my mind whirling with what to answer. "It's been, well, awkward living here with you. Having my own bedroom, while watching you two head into the master every night. But... it's been good too. And I want this. I really do." There was nothing I wanted more. "It's scary though, because I've never had a relationship before. Never had anyone *be* interested in a relationship with me. But it's also exciting, because I've fallen in love with the both of you."

A bit too early perhaps, but it was the truth. Well, not early to fall for Dion, as he'd been my teacher since last term had started. I'd seen him almost every day for months. Jeremy was a lot more sudden, but how could I not fall for him? He was such a caring person, always looking out for me.

"Was this what you expected?" Jeremy asked. "Being a part of our relationship, I mean?"

I shook my head slowly. Time to be honest. "I knew one thing: I wanted Dion. When I found out he had a boyfriend, I thought *fuck that*. I could just be on the side—as long as I could have him, I didn't give a shit. And my thoughts back then… it feels shitty now, after I've met you, but I never said I wasn't selfish. I wanted to take what I wanted—him—and screw whatever other factors were around."

I drew in a breath, stopping the flow of thoughts before I continued on and on. Maybe I was displaying manic symptoms? Surely the medicine must be out of my system by now. "So no, I hadn't expected this. I'd hoped Dion would feel enough for me to help me out after Dad beat me up, that I could stay for a couple of days before going back home. I never expected you, Jeremy—I never expected *this*."

It was more than I could've ever dreamt of.

"What about our places now?" Jeremy said, glancing between us. "I mean, if we're going to do this, all of us be together, we have to be together for real. And Dion, you and I, we are, but Chad has been on the outside. How are we supposed to—I don't know, figure out our *place*?"

What did he mean by place? I knew what place I was going to assume. "Neither of you like to be fucked, so I'm obviously going to be the bottom."

Jeremy strangled a surprised laugh. "That's not exactly what I meant, but okay." I could swear he was blushing. "Bed-arrangements have to be decided on too. You said yourself you feel awkward with us sharing a room together, and not with you. I can speak from experience now, and sharing a bed with you last night wasn't bad at all. If only the morning could've been equally good as the night before."

I could speak from experience too. If I hadn't jumped out of bed the minute I realised I hadn't had bloody morning wood that morning, we could've had a moment of waking up in bed together. But now, my traitorous body had to ruin what could've been a nice experience.

Well, Jeremy being late for work would've ruined it anyway, most likely, but still…

"So we're all going to share the master bed?" Dion scooted closer to us, so close our knees touched. "We all agree to that? I, personally, like the thought of that *a lot*."

Oh yeah.

"Yeah. Me too."

They smiled at each other, then looked at me. I all but vibrated where I sat. "I'd like that very much." I'd love it. I'd cherish it, I'd treasure it—I'd fuck the both of them until neither of them could move anymore. Because *that* was what I was good at, and that was what I was bringing to the relationship.

Dion leaned in and kissed me, which startled me because I hadn't seen it coming, but I quickly gave as good as I got. He had more stubble than Jeremy'd had last night, and it rasped even better against my skin.

A moan escaped me.

Funny, that, I hadn't even known I had a thing for stubble. *Just imagine what it must feel like in more intimate places on my body.* Just the thought made lust flash through me—and wouldn't you know, but I was getting *hard*.

I made a mental fist-pump at my dick not being ruined by the medicine, and then I practically jumped into Dion's lap, moulding myself to him.

Dion groaned, and for a moment I thought he lost his balance, but he braced both his arms on the floor behind him, which helped keep us both up. "Bloody hell." His eyes were shrouded though and his breathing went a bit faster than normal. He was turned on too.

I twisted my upper body around slightly so I could see Jeremy sitting at our sides. His gaze was locked on us, his lips parted a bit, and he seemed mesmerised for a moment—until he realised I'd turned to him, then he shook himself out of it.

"I got to admit—Seeing the two of you like that… that's hot."

"It would be even hotter if you came here too." I crooked a finger at him with a grin, then leaned over as he did as I said and kissed him passionately.

My arse rested comfortably in Dion's lap and I could feel his cock harden right up as I continued to kiss Jeremy deeply. Jeremy had one arm around my back now, keeping the two of us pressed close together, while the other grabbed for Dion's shoulder.

Dion, having gained his balance back, sat up properly again and wrapped his arms around us both, pulling all three of us in close. Then we were treated to another three-way kiss, lips on lips and tongue meeting tongues—and this was definitely the most intimate I had *ever* been with anyone. Everyone else I'd been with… it had just been sex, and sex had nothing to the sort of intimacy I currently felt at kissing the both of them at the *same time*.

I reached out with both my hands, as they were both free, and searched for the hem of their trousers. I had to loosen the zipper on Dion's, but Jeremy's was loose enough to slip my hand right down them, encountering hard cocks down both, straining against tight underpants.

Clothes were pulled down in a flurry, and then we all had our dicks out and we still kissed as we wanked each other off. I didn't even know which of them had his hand on my cock—all I knew was it felt wonderful.

I still straddled Dion's lap, and Jeremy was pressed in close to both our sides. There was so little space between us our hands brushed together as we stroked each other off.

Once my orgasm got close, I couldn't maintain the kiss, so I broke it and instead focused on what was going on further down. I had my hand on Dion's cock, Dion had his on Jeremy's, and Jeremy's on mine. It was amazing. The feeling of another's hand around me, seeing all our hands working each other, as well as the effect it had on our rock hard dicks—all three of them leaking pre-come like mad.

A tingling sensation started in my balls, and I cried out as I spurted all over Jeremy's hand and both his and my own trousers. My hand on Dion's cock stilled as I rode my own orgasm, and Dion quickened his speed on Jeremy, bringing him to climax as well.

I'd come down a bit while Jeremy rode out his, and I scooted back off Dion's lap and bent to swallow him down, making sure to keep my teeth behind my lips as I sucked him.

"Oh, fuck!" Dion's hips bucked up, forcing his cock further down my throat. Good thing I was an expert on deep-throating or I would've gagged.

I bobbed up and down, keeping my tongue along the underside of his cock. Dion's hand tangled in my hair, but he didn't force me down, just pulled a bit as I gave him the second best pleasure there was. The first was, obviously, to be buried in a tight arse. For him anyway. For me it was to *have* a cock buried deep in my arse.

He grunted as he came, and I swallowed what I could and made sure to lap up whatever managed to escape my lips.

"Bloody hell." Dion pulled me up to him and crushed his lips to mine, and I wrapped both arms and legs around him, holding him *tight, tight, tight*.

Then I remembered Jeremy, and I twisted around, threw my arms around his neck and drew him in for exactly the kind of crushing, hard kiss Dion had given me.

And the best thing of all?

He answered it.

And Dion's arms wrapped around us both again, bringing us in close—for yet another three-way kiss.

I could get used to this.

CHAPTER 14

*I*t was just as awkward to head to bed together, as it was for them to go into one room, while I had to take the other one.

Where was I going to sleep? What was their usual sleeping positions? What were their side of the bed?

Jeremy took the same side as he had last night, so I supposed that was his. Dion grinned at me, then lay down in the middle of it, leaving free space at his side for me to slide into.

Jeremy clicked off the light once I was in the bed and the duvet had been pulled up. I was in my boxers and a tee, as was Jeremy, while Dion slept in a bare chest. A very magnificent bare chest it was too, with a sprinkling of dark-blond hair all over it.

"Out there... That was good." It needed to be

said. We hadn't said anything after the incident, not even when we'd gone to clean up one after the other, but now in the darkness it was easier to speak about out loud. "It was *so* hot."

They both made grunting sounds of agreement.

It spurred me on, knowing they'd both enjoyed it. "So how come you've had proper sex if neither of you like to be fucked?"

"What do you mean proper sex?" Dion's head turned on the pillow, but it was so dark in the room we couldn't see each other. Or maybe my eyes just hadn't adjusted yet, which was also likely. "We don't have to have penetrative sex for it to be proper. You don't think earlier was *proper* sex?"

Well, when he put it that way. "Okay, good point. But seriously, you don't have anal sex at all?"

"Not really."

"But you like anal sex if you're the one doing the fucking?"

"Yeah, of course."

"Depends," Jeremy said on Dion's other side.

"Depends on what?" What could it possibly depend on?

"It's a messy affair, innit, so it depends on just how clean the person you're having penetrative sex with is." I could tell from the dip in the bed and from seeing his darker shape against the lighter one of the window that Jeremy pushed himself up on his elbows. "Personally, I don't like sticking my dick anywhere that hasn't been cleaned."

"Cleanliness is important then. But what if the sex happens spontaneously? Can't run off cleaning your arse in the middle of it, that would sure ruin the mood."

"In that case, there's not going to be any penetration." Jeremy's words were final, but in a friendly matter, not like he was brushing me off.

"Are you that squeaky about it?" I touched Dion's upper arm.

"Nah. If it gets messy, I just take a shower afterwards." He sounded more amused than anything. Amused about what, I didn't know.

"So I'm guessing you're also extremely vanilla?" They didn't sound like someone who had loads of kinky sex. Without anal sex, how much was there really left to do?

"Why? Are you extremely kinky?" It was Jeremy who answered, and he was chuckling.

"No, not really. I'll take a good, old-fashioned pounding every day, and I'll be a happy camper. There really is nothing better than a cock buried in my arse." I rolled onto my side and put my hand on Dion's arm, feeling his hard muscles and warm skin. "Have you both had some traumatic experiences with buttsex or what? Because really, it's amazing!"

"I haven't," Dion said. "I just don't like it. And I *have* tried it, so I know what I'm missing."

I hadn't been about to rub it in like that, but fair enough. You couldn't know what you didn't like until you'd tried it. That was my opinion anyway.

"Jeremy?"

"I wouldn't say traumatic," he started hesitantly, "but the times I've tried it, it's always been messy and it just... it turns me off. And as it doesn't feel particularly good, it isn't worth to endure it, at least not for me. I mean, I like fucking, of course I do, but everything just needs to be *clean*."

"Gotcha."

Dion slid his hand up my hip. "Talkative, much?"

"Are you tired?" I could take a hint.

"A bit, yeah. Got work in the morning."

Work. Yes. "I'm working the lunch shift. Guess I better get my beauty sleep too." I was keyed up though. Likely because things seemed to fall into place between us, and it made me all kinds of excited.

But I managed to dose off—until the ringing off the phone woke me up.

I stumbled out into the living room and grabbed

the landline. "'Lo?" I tried to rub the sleep from my eyes. I must've been out longer than it felt like.

"This is Sophia. Who am I speaking to?"

"Um, Chad." Spoken like I wasn't even sure of my own damn name. Well, sue me, I was tired and she'd woken me up. "It's the middle of the night."

"She's dead."

"Who?" Bloody hell, but my head seemed to be filled with cotton.

"Our mother."

"Oh." *Oh shit.* I hadn't even asked Dion about his meeting with his mum. Neither Jeremy nor I had, besides the initial question of why he'd been home so early. But he had said there'd been nothing for him there, so maybe he wasn't interested in sharing. "I'll get Dion. Wait a sec."

I padded barefoot back into the bedroom, where the both of them where still fast asleep.

I shook Dion lightly. "Dion? *Dion*?"

He groaned and turned over, swatting my hand away.

"Your sister's on the phone. Dion?"

He buried his face in his pillow, ignoring me completely. I got a feeling he wasn't a morning kind of person.

"It's about your mum. Dion!" I shook him harder, finally getting a reaction besides rejection.

"What?" He rolled onto his back, one arm thrown over his eyes.

"Your sister's on the phone. It's your mum."

"It's the middle of the bloody night." He sat up grudgingly.

It was on the tip of my tongue to say that people didn't stick to regular schedules when it came to dying, but I managed to filter myself before it actually slipped out.

I had *some* tact. This was his mum after all, no matter what he'd said about there being nothing for him back there.

"Fuck."

I could see him now, my eyes used to the darkness after sleeping, and he dragged his hands over his face.

"She's on the landline."

"Yeah, yeah, I'm coming," he murmured, and scooted to the edge of the bed. I watched his bare back disappear out the door, then I sat down cross-legged on my portion of the bed.

Going back to sleep would seem unfeeling, and I did want to know how he was doing after getting the news. It was one thing to say there was nothing there when his mum had still been alive—quite another when she actually died.

I'd been more relieved than anything when I'd

found out Dad had died—but maybe it would be different for Dion.

I didn't know, so I waited.

He came in, eventually, and all but fell back down in the middle of the bed. His face was turned to me, but his eyes were closed.

"Are you all right?" I watched him anxiously for any sign of... something. Grief, regret, hurt feelings. It was too dark to read expressions though, so I had no idea if any of them were present.

"Yeah."

"You sure?"

Jeremy rolled over on the other side of the bed, arm flopping over Dion's waist as he rested against his back. "Sure about what?" His voice was sleep-roughened.

"Mum died. Sophia just rang."

That woke Jeremy right up. "Shit. Are you all right?"

Dion made a sound that sounded like a mix between a snort and a chuckle. "Chad just asked the same thing. And yes, I told you there was nothing back there for me. I did promise Sophia I'd go to the funeral though. I hope you'll both go with me."

"Of course we will." Jeremy caressed the naked skin on Dion's back sleepily.

I still sat cross-legged, not quite sure what to do

with myself. He didn't seem sad over it, so trying to console him wouldn't work. He was too tired for sex. So what else was there to do for someone who'd just found out his mum was dead?

"Lay down, Chad." Dion pulled on my arm. "Go back to sleep."

"But... Are you sure you're okay?" I couldn't sleep if he was hurting.

"Yes. I'm fine. Sleep. Now." He managed to pull me down on the bed, and he wrapped one arm around my waist to keep me there.

I should trust he was fine when he said he was. Only thing he seemed to want to do was sleep, and I could respect that. I should get my sleep too, it was apparently important to get. If I even could go back to sleep now, that was.

Seemed I could, because when I woke up again the room was lit up and both Dion and Jeremy were gone. I lay on my back and listened, but everything was silent in the flat, so they both must've gone off to work.

Speaking of work... I was working the lunch shift, the busiest time of day in the Café. I didn't have to open, but I had to be early, so I should start to think about getting ready.

Today would also be the first day I wouldn't be

working with neither Harriet nor Jeremy. Jeremy worked the early shift at the pub.

I was supposed to work with Josh's boyfriend—and the one I'd threatened with a knife. If that wasn't cause for some major stress, I didn't know what was.

"Work, work, work," I muttered under my breath. I put my hands on my stomach, encountering something that was definitely *good* news.

Morning wood.

Now that felt wonderful to wake up to, didn't it? Especially after yesterday when I hadn't been able to get it up at all.

I slipped my hand down my boxers and wrapped my fingers around myself, closing my eyes as I started a slow stroke. Imagining the happenings of yesterday, of the three of us wanking off together, it didn't take me long to come.

Just imagining the feel of their hands on me, the sight of all our cocks being stroked to climax, of the intimacy we'd shared, was enough to get my blood boiling.

I came over the bottom part of my T-shirt, my come pooling onto the garment, slowly seeping into it and making a wet spot.

I got out of bed and headed into the bathroom, where I pulled the tee off and jumped into the shower. I hummed some tune I couldn't remember where I'd heard before as I cleaned myself and washed my hair.

Afterwards I brushed my teeth, got dressed, messed up my already messy hair, then headed into the kitchen to find something to eat. I had to eat before work, or I'd go the entire four hours with a rumbling stomach—and that was definitely not fun, especially when serving food to everyone else.

I stuffed my face as quickly as I could, then skipped out the door. Time for work. Time to work with someone whom I didn't know at all—and whom probably didn't *like* me at all.

Oh, this is going to be great fun.

CHAPTER 15

*T*hey were watching me.

Whenever I turned away, eyes were on me. Judging me, without having even spoken a word to me.

I'd muttered a hi to the both of them when I'd arrived, but I hadn't known what else to say. Especially not to the blond bloke I'd threatened with a knife last time I'd seen him. I couldn't even remember his bloody *name*.

And Josh's boyfriend... Well, I had sexually assaulted Josh, so he didn't like me either. He didn't so much as glance my way when I faced him, but when I turned, I could feel eyes digging into my back, into my neck.

Not to mention the guests. They watched me too,

if I was out front, their eyes following me around as I cleaned the available tables.

"Hey, pardon!"

I jerked around, seeing a man sitting alone at the table behind me. "Yes?"

"I ordered my sandwich without tomatoes, but the tomatoes are on." He pointed down at said sandwich, face set in a sour grimace.

I'd been standing next to Josh's boyfriend when he'd taken that order. "You didn't."

"Pardon me?" He started frowning.

"You didn't say you wanted it without tomatoes when you ordered." I definitely remembered him saying he only wanted the sandwich, whatever the hell the name of it was. But he had *not* said he wanted it without tomatoes.

"I did," he insisted, face back to the sour grimace. "I want a new one."

Something snapped.

I strode up to face him. "You *didn't*. And you're not getting a new one." I grabbed his plate and threw it at him, the sandwich flopping down onto his lap. "Eat your fucking food!"

As I strode back to the counter this time, Josh's boyfriend's eyes were finally on me when I was turned the right way.

"What?" I barked, brushing past him and into the

kitchen, where the blond bloke was busy with another order. He cast me a nervous glance, but I had no interest in him.

"That was a bit uncalled for, wasn't it?" Josh's boyfriend was in the doorway, arms crossed over his chest.

"If you don't like me, you can just say so," I snapped.

"What?" Now he frowned at me.

What was with everyone bloody staring at me when I was turned away and frowning when I faced them?

"I know you don't like me. Neither of you do." I pointed at each of them in turn to make my point. The blond-haired bloke turned to us, a look of surprise on his face. He also seemed apprehensive.

"Damian..."

Right, that was Josh's boyfriend's name. Still couldn't remember the blond's.

"You can stop looking at me. I know you have been. I can feel your eyes on me whenever I turn away. It's fucking creepy!"

"I'm going to ring Harriet." Damian brushed past me.

I grabbed onto his arm. "Why? Why do you have to ring her? She can't do anything."

"She can come get you." He wrestled his arm out of my grip.

"And you can go fuck off!" I shoved at him. "You going to ring Harriet up every time we work together? I know neither of you like me."

"We've never said that," the blond started, holding his palm up towards me. "Chad, really, we *do* like you. We don't have anything against you."

"Liars."

"Liars!"

They both stood stock still. Someone was yelling out front, but I couldn't hear what it was, and they didn't seem to care.

"You fucking liars!" I pointed accusingly at them. "What do you want from me? You keep staring at me, *leering*. What do you *want*?"

"They want you."

"They want to kill you."

"Dismember you."

"Shut up!" I pulled at my hair.

"Chad." Damian came closer again, but he was wary. "Let me ring Harriet, or 999. Let me ring someone. You can't be here right now."

"They don't think you can take care of yourself."

"You can't take care of yourself, can you?"

"You're not ringing anyone! I'm not a fucking child!" I lifted my head in time to see Damian jerk his head at the blond, who nodded quickly and slinked away. "Don't you dare!"

Anger pulsed inside me and I lunged for him, only to be stopped by Damian's arms locking around my upper body. My arms were crushed to my sides and I trashed. "Let me go, you arsehole! Fucking *let me go!*"

I managed to get out of his grip—by possibly kicking him in places that really shouldn't be kicked—and I jumped out of his reach. "I'm so fucking out of here. And don't you dare ring, Harriet!"

He was crouched over and I ran out of the Café before he could get a hold of me again.

Nosy, nosy people, trying to make decisions for me.

I was my own damn master—and there was nothing they could do about it.

I eventually found myself at home—at my dad's house, and as nothing had happened with it yet, I still had the key. I didn't bother locking the door once I was inside, because really, who would bother coming in here? And if they did, they could steal whatever they wanted. It wasn't like I wanted to keep anything.

The sofa called to me and I sat down cross-legged on it, staring down at the floor beneath me.

That's where they found him. The bastard.

"Don't you dare call me names, you little piece of shite!"

I jerked, expecting a hit, but nothing happened.

Glancing around, I fully expected to see Dad standing there, raging at me, but I saw nothing.

"You're dead. You're not here. You're not alive." Another glance down at the carpet and the spot there. I wasn't sure if it had been there before he died or not. *I hope you rot.*

"Chad. Chad, Chad, Chad. Chadchadchadchad."

Whimpering, I curled in on myself, holding my hands pressed over my ears. It didn't help, I could still hear the voices. I fell sideways, until I was lying down on the sofa instead of sitting. Voices were trying to talk over each other, and I couldn't catch any coherency in it. I continued to press my palms to my ears, but they were equally as loud as if I hadn't done it.

I didn't know how long I laid there.

The voices stopped after some time, so all I could hear was silence... and footsteps on the floor.

I tensed, knowing I wouldn't stand a chance if it really was someone breaking in, someone with ill-intensions.

"You twat." I was whacked over the head, then pushed up into a sitting position. Wynn's face was in front of me all of a sudden and then he was shaking me. "You said you'd go back on your medicine."

"I did." I hadn't. I hadn't even taken the mood stabilisers today, now I thought about it. "I forgot."

"Obviously." Wynn sat down next to me, so close I could lean on him.

"That's where Dad died." I stared down at his feet. "Or that's where they found him, anyway, so I suppose that's where he died. Unless someone moved him."

"Unless you're in an episode of bloody CSI, I doubt someone's been in and moved him." His voice bled of sarcasm. "Are you paranoid?"

"What? No."

"That's a manic symptom. See, I've read up on it, so now I can see the symptoms for what they are, instead of assuming they're drugs."

"I haven't done drugs since..." Since when? "Since the last time I did them."

"Very profound, Chad." He clapped me on the shoulder. "That makes it real easy for me to pinpoint the exact time since you've taken any."

"I don't remember, ok? It was at your place, anyway. Maybe before the hospital? Or after... I don't know."

"But you haven't taken any recently?"

I shook my head against his shoulder.

"Good."

"Have *you*?" I didn't want for him to have an overdose again. Maybe this time around he wouldn't survive.

"No." It came out on a sigh. "I'm not going back to that bloody hospital."

"That doesn't mean you're not still using." I wrapped my arms around his middle. "I don't want you to die."

"And I don't want you to die, and you're at risk for that if you get manic. So you need to take your medicine."

"I got a new prescription of antipsychotic."

"Then use it," he insisted.

I was afraid to. "What if it fucks everything up again? What if I can't have sex again, huh? What if it doesn't even work, because the dosage is too low, and I have to be on the dosage I had, which makes everything down there shrivel up. I can't *do* that."

"You'd rather be manic with a sex-drive than calm without one?"

"*Yes.*" It wasn't even a contest. I liked being happy. Today I hadn't been, today had been complete shit, but I used to be. Until I crashed, but at least I had the good moments to think back on.

Wynn snorted. "You're mental is what you are."

"That has been proven now, yes. Rapid-cycling bipolar I with psychotic features. It's a right laugh." Except I couldn't laugh about it now. Maybe I was already crashing down. Maybe I was depressed. Maybe it was my turn to end up catatonic in a bed without being able to measure up the will or the strength to do anything. I'd been like it before, exactly like Wynn had been—and I knew I would be again.

I listened to Wynn's even breathing for a while, until he spoke again.

"I'd take the tablets and the after-affects in front of not being able to take care of myself." It came out in a low voice, like he was admitting a shameful secret. Maybe to him it was shameful. "I don't want to be the person who spends days, weeks, maybe even months in bed because I can't face reality. Reality is that Madison is dead—and you almost died, and I did too. It's a reality I have to face, if I want to or not. If I couldn't... then what is there to live for anymore?"

My blood ran cold. I'd heard that pondering question before—in my own damn mind. When I'd considered jumping from the bridge right into the Thames, and a lot of other times in my life too.

"You don't get to die, you hear me?" I hugged him tighter, as tight as I was able to. "You're my best mate. Just because Madison was selfish, you don't get to be."

He drew in a sharp breath—and I realised I might've said too much. No one spoke bad of Madison, *ever*.

But Wynn relaxed again against me, and he let the subject drop without comment.

I was grateful for that, because I honestly didn't feel like being beat up—like people had been when they made fun of Madison when they'd been back in college.

Wynn could be extremely violent, but only to protect someone he loved. He loved me too though, which was proven by him simply dropping the subject like he had.

"I don't know what I would've done without you. All these years... you've been the only one there for me, no matter what."

"I've been the only one you haven't pushed away, rather. You could've had your aunt—but you didn't want to confide in her."

"She would've gone to the police."

"I should've done that too."

"Dad gave me a roof over my head, at least."

"While beating you up." Wynn wasn't going to let it lie.

"Yes, but... if Harriet had gone to the police when

I was younger, I would've been given into her custody, and I couldn't bring *this* on her." I motioned to myself in general. "You've always understood me, but I didn't think she would. I didn't even know mum was bipolar until I was in hospital myself. I didn't know that's why she'd died."

"Killed herself, you mean."

A beat of silence. "Yeah." If I hadn't been facing away from the kitchen, my eyes would've gone that way, to the place where I'd found her lying in her own blood.

"People keep dying on us." It was a true observation.

"No one else." I buried my face against his shoulder. "No one else is going to fucking die. I forbid it."

He chuckled bitterly. "That goes for you, as well. Go back on your medicine."

"I will. I promise."

"You already have promised me—and you've already broken it. So sue me if I don't believe you this time around."

True enough. "You can walk back home to the flat with me, and you can tell Dion and Jeremy. They'll make sure I take my meds."

"Now that's not too shabby an idea." Wynn stood so abruptly I almost face planted on the cushions. "Come on."

"I didn't mean right now," I complained.

"Now's as good a time as any." He held his hand out—and after a beat of hesitation, I took it. He hauled me to my feet, dropped my hand, and instead squished my face between both of his. "You'll be all right. You just have to take the prescribed medicine, and then everything'll be right."

"I hear people say that," I said through my squished cheeks. "But I've also read that rapid-cycling bipolar is the most difficult to treat, and the one that responds the least to medicines."

"Then do whatever you have to do. You *have* to be okay. For your aunt, for your blokes—and for me." His gaze was uncharacteristically soft, almost begging me. And Wynn didn't beg anyone for *anything*.

"I will," I promised, my throat closing up in emotion. "I *will*."

"Good. Now let's get you home." He dragged me across the floor, allowed me time to lock the door, then down the stairs, and onto the kerb.

I stopped once we were there to stare back at the house. "I've lived in this house my entire life."

"And what a shit life it's been." Wynn didn't hold back. He never did.

I like that about him.

"Yeah." I couldn't remember much from when

Mum had been alive, but it must've been better then. Right? After she was gone, it'd all turned into a right hell. A hell that was now finally over.

I had a new home now—a home with two wonderful blokes who liked me, no matter how much of a mess it had all been in the beginning.

And I... I was in love with them both, and if I didn't get my act together I could lose them both before even having them properly.

I didn't want to lose them, or Harriet now we'd got closer, and definitely not Wynn. I didn't want to lose anyone, and to stop that from happening I had to get better. I had to do my best.

For all of them—but also for myself.

PART IV
DION

CHAPTER 16

There was an incessant knocking on the door.

I'd just got home from work, had managed to change into the comfortableness of joggers and a T-shirt, when someone banged on our front door.

"Can you get that?" Jeremy yelled from the kitchen.

"Yeah!" I strode over, curious to what was the big emergency. When I opened it, I was met with someone dressed all in black.

"He's off his meds." Wynn drew a slouching Chad in front of him. "Get him back on his new dosage *now*." He all but shoved Chad into my arms, then buggered off without even so much as a glance back.

I got Chad into the flat by holding an arm around him, while I closed the door with the other one. He toed his shoes off and shrugged out of his jacket, which I hung up, then shuffled by my side over to the sofa, where he fell down.

I stood at the side of it, staring down at him. "Is it true? You're off your medicine?"

He closed his eyes and turned his head away, towards be back of the sofa. "I had to."

"Why? Why would you possibly go off your medicine?" It wasn't healthy to go off the meds suddenly—not for his mind, which could spiral again, and not for his body. I'd read about it, and every article had warned about suddenly stopping medication.

"Sex. I couldn't do it when I was on them."

I froze.

We'd had sex the day before, which meant he'd been off his medication then as well.

"What's going on?" Jeremy came out of the kitchen, drying his hands on a kitchen towel.

"He's off his meds."

Jeremy peered over the back of the sofa, down at Chad who by now had turned on his side so he was lying with his back to me. "Why?"

"Because he wanted to have sex with us, and he apparently couldn't while on the medicine." *Jesus,*

Chad. I wanted to shake him, tell him how stupid he was for going off his meds like that, but I couldn't get myself to do it. I couldn't even get myself to tell him, because I knew it would sound accusative and he was clearly depressed already. I couldn't make it worse.

Jeremy put the kitchen towel down, then braced both hands on the back of the sofa. "What happened today, Chad?"

Good question.

"I messed up." It came out so mumbled it was hard to tell the words apart. "People kept staring at me, and one customer was a right arse, so I threw his sandwich at him. Then I think I kicked Damian in the… in the nuts."

A sympathetic chill went through me. "Why'd you do that?"

"Because he held me back. That blond bloke was going to go ring Harriet and I couldn't let that happen, so I was going to stop him, but he stopped *me*, so I kicked him. I didn't mean to kick him there, it just—it just happened."

That was two incidents in the Café in approximately just as many weeks. "Maybe you shouldn't be working right now, Chad. Maybe you should just focus on therapy and finding the exact right medication that works for you?"

"I can't. I need money."

"Why?" Wasn't his mental health more important? "You have a place to live, food's provided. If there's something you need, we can get it for you. I've got a steady income—and now that Jem's working at the Café, he's earning more too. We'll be fine economically."

"I can't live off of you!" He sat up so suddenly I took a step back in surprise, and the depression was gone for now, replaced by anger. "I can't *do* that! I need to be able to care for myself!"

"You can get benefits, until you can try and get back into employment. There's possibilities out there, without you having to stress so much now when you're in the initial phase of diagnosis. What's most important for you right now is to find the right medicine and the right dosage, so you can function properly." I had to get through to him. "You can't work when it leads to incidents like today. Not even Harriet's going to allow it. You threatened Leslie with a knife once, and today you tried to attack him? You need to sort yourself out before you can start working."

Anger bled away, and he dissolved into fitful sobbing.

Jeremy stared at me for a moment, startled and shocked at the range of emotions we'd seen so far, then he was around the sofa and sat next to Chad. "Hey, come on. *Shhh*." He rubbed his back soothingly.

I sat on the arm of the sofa, watching Jeremy's hand soothe over Chad's bent back. "Chad, you just need a break. I'm not saying you can't ever work, but I think that right now what's best for you is to take it easy."

"I don't want to be like this!" He leaned into Jeremy's chest, his words choked out between sobs. "I don't want to act like I do, but I can't help it! I don't want this!" He lashed out, but Jeremy grabbed his wrists before he could do any harm and forced them in close to his body.

Chad's sobs got louder, almost drowning out the sound of more knocking on the door.

This knocking wasn't as loud and incessant as Wynn's had been earlier, but that didn't mean he couldn't be back.

He wasn't.

Harriet stood outside, face set in a serious expression as she looked up at me. "Wynn said he brought Chad back here."

"You've been speaking to Wynn?" I'd had the impression she didn't care much for Chad's best friend.

"After Leslie rang me and told what happened at

the Café, I figured Wynn would have a better chance at finding him and calming him down than I could." She drew in a deep breath, her head cocking to one side. "Is that him?"

The sobs could be heard loud and clear from where we were standing. "Yeah." I stepped out of the way so she could come in, and hurried over to the sofa with a look of worry. "Chad?"

Jeremy focused on her, but not Chad. He was still hunched over, face buried against Jeremy's chest as he cried his heart out.

I took my seat at the arm of the sofa again, then leaned down to brush a light caress over Chad's shoulder. "I know it seems unfair, but once you find the right medicine, it'll be easier."

He shook his head violently, but didn't seem to be able to speak. Jeremy had stopped rubbing his back and instead just kept his arms wrapped around him.

"Oh, Chad." Harriet watched him sadly, but also with a far-away look, which told me she'd experienced this too before, probably with either her sister or father, or both.

"How's your employee?" I asked her. "He got a good kick in his private parts."

"Who?" She blinked in surprise. "Damian didn't say anything about that, just that Chad was acting manic. And that he left." She glanced at Chad's bent back, uncertain now. "They would've told me if either of them were actually hurt. I hope." A frown line marred her eyebrows.

Chad had quieted down a bit, but he didn't move from his position. He was still sniffling and his body shook every time he hiccupped.

"Chad?" She leant over and put a hand on his shoulder. "Do you want me to stay?"

He shook his head in answer, and Harriet straightened with a sad look.

"I think he just needs some good rest," I said as I followed her back to the door.

She blew out a breath. "He shouldn't come to work tomorrow. Keep him home. I'll manage on my own. I did before too. Just… Just keep him safe." Her eyes were begging me when she looked up at me. "That kind of depression, with the tears and the hopelessness and the complete negativity… that's how Kendra was the last time I saw her. Next I knew she'd taken her own life. I don't—that *can't* happen to him."

"It won't." I'd sit with him all bloody night if need be, but that promise was one I intended to keep. "I promise, Harriet, as long as he's here with us, nothing will happen to him."

She nodded jerkily, gaze flickering back to Chad and Jeremy. "Take care of him."

"We will. The best care." Anything else wouldn't be acceptable.

She left, seemingly even more emotional than when she'd arrived, and I went back to the sofa.

"I have to check the food." Jeremy gazed up at me. "Will you sit with him?"

We switched places, and I took a pillow from the other end of the sofa to put on my lap, then I gently pushed him down in a lying position. It would be better for him than the hunched over position he'd been in.

"I can't do this," he whispered.

"Yes, you can." I stroked my hand through his thick, coarse hair. "You're strong. I know you can do anything."

"No. I really can't." His voice was thick, and I swore I could see more tears gathering from what I could see of one eye. "I can't do anything properly."

"Bollocks, Chad." I bent down and placed a kiss on his temple. "You're a very good artist." Though at that, I hadn't seen him draw in any of his sketch-books in a while. Maybe that was because of the rapid-cycling?

He didn't answer, and I sat there, my hand continuing to stroke through his hair, as I listened to Jeremy move around in the kitchen.

He soon came out with three plates, which he put

down on the coffee table.

"I made shepherd's pie." His gaze flicked to Chad, who didn't move. "It's my mum's recipe—I practically grew up on this."

My mouth watered and my stomach rumbled. I loved Jeremy's shepherd's pie. "Come on, love, you need to eat." I coaxed Chad up into a sitting position, but he only leant against the back of the sofa, not even eying the food.

Jeremy sat down on my other side, worried and unsure of what to do.

I didn't know what to do either, so I just started in on the food. Maybe if we ate, he'd be tempted too.

"His meds," Jeremy said all of a sudden. "He has to take his meds." And he hurried into the bathroom to get them.

He'd forgotten to bring drinks out with the food, so I headed into the kitchen to get that, pouring cold water from the tap.

By the time I got back to the sofa, and Jeremy got back from the bathroom, Chad was crying again.

"What's wrong?" I put the glasses down, then went over to rub his back and shoulders.

"I didn't hear Mum today," he hiccupped. "I use to hear Mum when I hear voices, but I didn't today. I heard Dad, and other people, and they said bad things. It wasn't anything *good*."

"All the more reason to take your medicine." Jeremy crouched down in front of him, two tablets in the palm of his hand. "The voices will go away as long as you take them."

"But I want to hear my *mum*!"

"It's not really her, Chad. She's dead. It's all in your head." I wasn't sure if that would be too forward for him, but he knew his mum had died long ago, so he must also know that if he heard her voice... it was only in his own mind, thanks to his disorder. It wasn't something that was *real*.

He started sobbing again, burying his face in his hands.

"*Shhh*." I wrapped my arms around him and rested my cheek against the back of his head. "Take your medicine and this will all get better."

We stayed like that, me holding him and Jeremy crouched in front of him, until he'd cried himself out. Then he willingly, albeit slowly, took the tablets and swallowed them with the glass of water Jeremy held out to him.

He still didn't eat, just sat listlessly on the sofa next to us, and Jeremy and I emptied our own plates and shared his one between us as well.

Couldn't let Jeremy's shepherd's pie go to waste, after all.

CHAPTER 17

FIVE DAYS LATER

*B*ack in my hometown once again, for the second time in a week.

That fact was even more depressing than what we were even there for. My mum's funeral, to be held early the next day, which was why we'd decided to spend the night here.

I regretted it already.

"This isn't too shabby." Jeremy dumped his bag on the double bed in our hotel room.

"I've never been in a hotel before." Chad stuck his head into the bathroom, then came over to feel the spread on the bed. He sat down on it, jumping up and down a couple of times like a little kid. "Motels are nothing like this."

"Motels?" How could he have afforded that?

"Well, yeah. Lots of blokes don't want to bring a trick home, you know." He said it unashamedly—and I suppose to him sex with random blokes had been a part of life. "They're rather take in on a hotel for an hour, get it done, then they're off."

Jeremy grimaced, but he was on the other side from Chad, so he didn't see it. "That doesn't sound very… fulfilling."

"Hey, it's sex." Chad fell back on the bed, arms spread wide. "It's always good. Well, okay, not always. Most of the time though, if the bloke knows what he's doing. I've had a couple who was all about putting it in right away, without preparation or lube. Some think spit's enough. Let me tell you, it's *not*."

Chad had been getting better in the last four days, and today he was rather perky. I hoped it was the medicine kicking into full effect and not him spiralling back up into mania.

"This bed's wider than yours." He spread his arms further, without being able to touch the edges. "This'll be comfortable."

"Our bed isn't comfortable?" I put my own bag down on the floor, out of the way so no one would trip over it.

"Well, yeah, but it's narrower, and with three people in it, it can be a bit crowded at night. I've noticed you tend to take up bigger space once you're asleep."

"I do not."

"You do." He grinned cheekily at me. "The minute you're off you just spread out."

"I don't believe you." I looked to Jeremy, who met my gaze straight on. "Do I?"

"You kind of do. You also don't like to cuddle when you're asleep."

"I get hot," I defended myself. I couldn't stand sleeping close to anyone—spooning in bed or have someone halfway atop me, it just made me feel over-heated. I needed space when I slept, which might be why I *took* more space, so no one would get too close. "Anyway." I was done with this subject. "Are you ready to head back out?" We were meeting Sophia for dinner at a restaurant in town. It was popular, apparently, so she'd even reserved us a table.

Back when I'd lived here, nowhere had been popular enough to reserve anything. Maybe more people had moved to town since I'd been gone, or the ones who lived here had become more outgoing.

"How does it feel, being back here?" Jeremy asked once we were out of the hotel and heading down the street. "Does it bring back a lot of bad memories?"

"Not really." I didn't think about my past walking

down the street. The town itself didn't hold any bad memories, per say. But if I saw my childhood home again, then it would be another matter. "I've got no plans showing you where I grew up though. I got enough of that house before I even left, and the quick visit I had last week... it was more than enough."

"I guess that's fair."

"Did you grow up in a small town too?" Chad asked Jeremy.

"I grew up just outside of London, in the suburbs."

A childhood the opposite of both Chad's and mine. With parents who were happy together and who had loved him more than anything. Maybe that's where Jeremy had learned to be so caring, and so forgiving. I was still in awe by the fact that we were all three of us together. That Jeremy had forgiven me cheating on him with Chad, and that he'd taken care of Chad when he'd been hurt, and now allowing him into our relationship.

It was all more than I could've ever dreamt of.

And it was wonderful.

~

"So, Sophia, do you have anyone special in your life?" I knew her tendency to not elaborate, so I'd waited with the personal questions until our food had arrived, so it wouldn't be so many awkward silences with nothing else to do.

"No."

"Are you married?"

"No."

"Have a boyfriend? Girlfriend?"

"No."

Her expression didn't change in the slightest as she kept rebuffing my questions. She ate her food calmly, and nothing seemed to be bothering her. Seemed she was perfectly happy being alone.

"Do you have any pets then?" Was she really *all* alone? It sounded horrible to me, after those first few years after I left home when I *had* been truly alone. But then her and I were quite different people.

"No."

It was hard to keep a conversation going when she only answered with one-syllable words and didn't reciprocate on the questions. It grated on me a bit—because we hadn't seen each other in fifteen years, after all. Wasn't she a little bit curious what my life was like?

"Is there anything you want to ask me?"

She blinked, taken by surprise. "Is there anything you want me to ask you?" It was like she was searching for the right answer.

"I don't know, Sophia. It's been over a decade, and yet you don't ask about my life, or share anything about yours."

"I'm a solicitor, you're a teacher. I'm single, you're spoken for. *Twice*." She cast a pointed look at both Jeremy and Chad, who'd stayed quiet up till now. "You live in London, I live here. What else is there?"

I gave up. There was no point.

"Nothing. That covers basically everything." My voice was laced with irony, but she only nodded as if happy with that statement. That too was no change from when we were young. She didn't *get* irony. "Everything set for the funeral tomorrow?" I asked instead, moving the conversation along.

"Yes."

But yeah, it wasn't easy to actually get a conversation going.

~

"It's almost full," Jeremy whispered, glancing behind us at the rows upon rows of people.

I'd already noticed. "I didn't know my mum was this popular." Before I'd buggered off, she hardly ever went out of the house.

"She got out more once Dad died." It was like Sophia read my bloody mind. "Started going to

Bingo and to this group with other ladies where they knit together."

That was probably the longest sentence I'd heard from her since we'd arrived yesterday. And it was explanatory too, which wasn't her strong point.

"That... nice." Maybe she'd finally felt free after Dad was put in the ground, and finally found her proper place. By going to bingo and knitting. Not the most productive things, in my mind, but if she'd enjoyed it... I didn't hold any love for her, but if her last years had been happy, then that was good.

"You okay?" Jeremy leaned sideways so our shoulders bumped together. Chad peered at me curiously from Jeremy's other side.

"I'm fine." I could do with not sitting on the hard benches, as they hurt my arse, or listen to a priest preach on about someone he didn't even know—or at least I suppose he didn't, unless Mum had found religion in the last fifteen years.

The service started, and I ended up drowning out whatever the priest droned on about—and then Chad started laughing. And not just a low chuckle, but full out laughter where he even bent over.

I turned, slow-motion, to stare at both him and Jeremy. "Is he off his meds?" It was the first thing that fell into my mind.

Jeremy licked his lips. "I don't think so. Maybe they're not working."

"Off my meds—" Chad turned his face towards us, still laughing. It was drawing attention. "Is that the solution to everything, huh? I'm going mental—I must be off my meds."

"What's so funny?" I snapped in a low voice. People were turning towards us now, wanting to know the source of the interruption.

"This!" Chad motioned to the front of the church, the priest and the coffin and *everything*. "I fucked a priest in a church much like this. Right up there, by the alter. It was *fantastic*!"

Surely this couldn't be the same man who took advantage of a grieving eleven year old boy. If I ever got my hands on him, I'd wring his neck, no matter if Chad thought about it fondly or not.

I stood and squeezed past Jeremy, then grabbed Chad around the waist and hauled him with me.

"What are you doing?" He squirmed in my grip, but he was still laughing.

"We're going outside." I dragged him with me down the entire isle, with every single eye on us on the way.

Jeremy followed close behind—and once we were out in the gravel driveway, I saw Sophia had come too.

"You can go back in. You don't have to miss Mum's funeral for this."

It was like I'd flipped a switch. The laughter cut off and Chad turned with bloody murder in his eyes. "I'm not worth missing a funeral over? That what you think?"

"She doesn't know you." It hadn't been what I meant. Well, for Sophia it had, but what was more important to me was *him*. "This hasn't got anything to do with her."

He stared at me, eyes intense and dark. "She's your sister. She's practically family."

"Dion…" Jeremy came in close to me. "He's rapid cycling. But I swear, I've seen him take his medicine every day."

So his new dosage was too low. If he hadn't been depressed for the last days, it might've been caught sooner, but depression was part of the disorder that couldn't be treated properly—as medicine for the depressed part induced the manic part of it.

"Bloody hell." I dragged my hands through my hair and over my face in frustration.

"If I'm such a bother, why do you even fucking *bother*?" Chad stalked off, down the gravel driveway. He didn't get far though before he all but fell down on the kerb, curling in on himself.

TT KOVE

I closed my eyes and took a few steadying breaths.

"He can't help it."

Of course I knew that. It was just that we were back here, in this place filled with shitty things, the place I'd run from, burying the person who'd been nothing but a shitty mother. And I didn't need Chad to act out.

"Here's my keys." Sophia was in front of me, thrusting said keys into my hand. "Take him back to the hotel."

Miss the funeral. Well, it wasn't like I was attached to it anyway. "Thanks."

"You're welcome." She nodded gruffly, then went back inside without another word.

Both Jeremy and I stared after her, then we turned in unison towards Chad, who was still at the kerb.

"Will you get the car, and I'll get him?" I handed the keys over to Jeremy, who took them somewhat hesitantly.

My shoes crunched against the gravel. "Hey." I crouched in front of him. "Come on, we're going back to the hotel."

"I don't know why you bother with me," he choked out. "I ruin everything. I'm sorry. I'm so sorry."

"*Shhh.*" I stroked his hair, then grabbed both of

200

his shoulders and dragged him up to a standing position. I heard the car start up, and wheels on gravel as Jeremy backed it out, then he drove slowly down towards us. "Of course we bother. That's why we're here. That's why *I'm* here."

The car came to a halt besides us and Jeremy got out to open the back door.

"You said I'd get better." He was crying now, his chest heaving with painful sobs. "You said, as long as I took my medicine, I'd feel *better*!"

"You need a stronger dosage." I pulled him into my arms, cradling his head against my collarbone. "We'll go home tomorrow and you can see your psychiatrist and your doctor. They have to fix it for you."

Jeremy came up behind Chad, hands flicking over his back in worry before he hugged him from the other side so Chad was sandwiched between us.

"You are going to feel better. You just have to find the right medicine for you."

I believed it too.

But it was easier said than done.

CHAPTER 18

J went back to the cemetery that evening, as a feeling came over me that I needed to see the grave.

The dirt was piled high on it with only a cross signalling it was Mum's grave in the first place. Flowers and wreaths and ribbons covered most of the dirt, making sure the pile stood out from the rest of the cemetery, where every other grave had sunk and green grass was the only thing to be seen besides all the various headstones.

I crouched down by the head of the grave. As far as I knew, Mum hadn't ever had any friends. How come so many had been in the church, and how come her grave was all filled up with all of this?

"Did you regret it, Mum?" I didn't know why I

spoke out loud. It wasn't like she was there to answer for herself, and the day I'd *had* the chance to talk to her, I'd left. "How you treated us? How you let Dad treat us? Treat *you*?" Had she truly realised the error of her ways or had she simply been a selfish bitch to the end?

It didn't quite explain why she'd wanted to see me—and now it was too late, I'd never find out.

My chest was tight as memories from my childhood came flashing back. Of all the yelling and the fighting and the beatings. Of walking home from school and seeing Dad out with some young, big-tits and arse bimbo, pawing all over her in his horniness to get in her knickers.

"I'm not like Dad." It came out a whisper. "I cheated on Jeremy, but it all worked out... we're all together. I'm *not* like him." I'd always been afraid of it. I'd always promised myself I'd stay faithful to my partner—but I'd broken it by sleeping with Chad, by hurting Jeremy, and generally messing everything up before it'd come together.

But if Jeremy hadn't fallen for Chad... what would've become of us then? Would he have been able to forgive me if Chad had been out of the picture? If he'd never shown up on our door that day, Jeremy never would've let him in, never would've started to worry about him. Where would we be if that were the case?

"Did you ever forgive that?" She couldn't have. Not for the cheating, not for the beatings. She'd spent most of our lives in bed, for god's sakes. It seemed she'd only got out of it once the old man had died.

"Why are you talking to yourself? She's dead. She can't answer you."

I jumped approximately ten feet in the air at the voice coming from behind me, then turned to glare at my sister. "You could've announced your presence, instead of nearly giving me a heart attack."

"Are you liable for those?" And there she went, taking my word for it.

"No." I shook my head. "Figure of speech."

"Oh."

She was in running clothes. "You run past the graveyard every day?" Must be depressing.

"No. But I stopped by your hotel room, and your lovers said you'd be here."

"Boyfriends," I corrected. That's what they were, the both of them.

Her eyebrows rose. "But you do have sex together?"

"Well, yeah."

"Then they're also your lovers."

I wasn't even going to argue about definitions.

She was technically right, after all, though lovers weren't a term I preferred to use.

"What's wrong with the redheaded one? He was acting weird in church."

I swallowed the initial laughter that threatened to burst. "Acting weird is putting it mildly. He's bipolar. Hasn't found the right kind of medicine and dosage yet." I hoped he'd find it soon. Not for us, but for him. The rapid-cycling grated even more on his psyche than it did on us.

And as long as he was cycling from one constant to the next, we could never settle down, the three of us. We could never find our footing, until he'd found *his*.

"Does it ever bother you?" I glanced back at the grave.

"Does what bother me?"

"How they treated us. That they never realised the errors of their ways." I liked to believe if I'd been like them, I would've realised what a bastard I was sooner or later. Surely they had to? They couldn't keep being such selfish, psychopathic people for the majority of their lives, could they? When they'd driven one child away and the other likely couldn't be bothered to have much to do with them. But then, again, that was just Sophia's personality.

"Why would they? It's who they were. People

don't change that easily." She put it out there, in a straight-forwardness that I'd only ever heard from her.

I sighed. "Maybe you're right."

"I *am* right." It didn't even occur to her that she could be wrong. In this instance, I was likely to take her word for it. She'd stayed here the past fifteen years, she'd known them, whereas I had no idea what they'd been like. "They never changed. Just like I never changed, and I'm sure you never changed."

"I've changed." I cast her an affronted glare. "I've changed a lot. I'm not the gangly, afraid teenager I was when I ran away."

"You've grown more confident, but underneath it all you're still exactly the same. That goes for everyone. You can never change who you are."

I didn't believe that. I believed a person *could* change, if they realised the errors of their way and really made an effort. But I didn't want to argue with her. These were her views, and I had different ones. We had different personalities—it was just the way it was.

"When are you leaving?" She swiftly changed the subject.

"Tomorrow. Once we get up and ready." I didn't want to stay any longer than I absolutely *had* to. If Chad hadn't been rapid cycling today of all days, I would've preferred to go home after the funeral. But taking a rapid cycling Chad on the train... that was a disaster waiting to happen.

Sophia thrust her hand out and I stared at it in confusion. "This is goodbye then." She jerked it closer to me, and I was forced to shake it.

"Not proper goodbye, I hope?" I frowned at her. "We'll keep in touch?"

"If you want us to."

"I do." I didn't want to abandon my little sister again. I wanted her to stay a part of my life from now on, now we'd actually met again.

Besides, she'd admitted she didn't have anyone special in her life, and when we'd been kids she'd never been any good at making friends... so I was pretty sure she didn't have anyone there for her.

I think I surprised her more than even myself when I drew her into a tight hug. She was stiff against me, hands hanging down by her sides, but I continued to hold her close for another minute. She'd just have to deal. "I'm glad you found me."

She cleared her throat, but didn't say anything. When I finally let her go, she took a step back.

"I don't want us to stop speaking. When I ran away... I didn't want to have anything to do with this place anymore, but you're my sister and you're the only one I've been thinking about. I've wondered all these years what happened to you, if you were mad at me for leaving without a word."

"I'm not. You made a choice, and you stuck with it. Good for you." She was clearly uncomfortable now, but I didn't think it had anything to do with me. It was more her trying to understand me, as she was exceptionally bad at understanding other people.

"Thank you for understanding. Though it was shitty of me to never contact you." It grated on me, but it didn't seem to face her much. "If you're ever in London, stop by. If you ever just want to talk, you ring me. And I'll do the same."

She nodded slowly, gaze flickering thoughtfully.

I didn't hold out any hope it would happen, at least not her calling me, but at least I'd put it out there. The offer would always stand, and I hoped she realised that.

WHEN I CAME BACK to the hotel room, it was dark and empty.

I wondered where they'd gone off too, but I was too tired from the entire day to ponder it for long. The minute I stretched out on the bed, I was out of it.

I woke groggily to being prodded gently.

"Move over," Chad whispered. "You're hogging the whole bed."

I rolled onto my side with a groan, eyes too heavy to even open them. "Where've you been?" I wasn't sure the question came out any sort of understandable.

"We went for a walk. There was this lovely trail, away from the bustle of civilisation."

So my question had been understandable anyway. And Chad sounded excited and happy.

I dropped my shoulder back down on the bed so I was on my back again and forced my eyes open to peer at him. "You getting manic again?"

He stared down at me, green eyes sincere. "I don't think so."

"The walk calmed him down." Jeremy came into my line of vision now too, smiling at Chad and clapping him on the shoulder. "And cheered him up."

"The nature's calming. It's not the bustle of people all around and the sound of vehicles everywhere you turn. It was quiet—except for the birds." Chad smiled too, and it warmed my heart to see. He turned sombre once he glanced back down at me though. "I'm so sorry about the funeral. You missed it, and I... it was so stupid."

I reached out for his hand, then pulled him down on the bed for a chaste kiss. "It's okay, Chad. As long as you're feeling better, that's all that matters." His skin and clothes were cold against my sleep-warmed self, so it must be getting late and drafty outside.

"How was seeing her grave?" Jeremy sat down on the bed now too, against my hip, and his hand spread out on my lower stomach.

"Didn't really do anything this way or that for me. She's gone. I can't ever get the answers I need." I think I was okay with that. Mostly. I didn't think she'd ever give me the answers I needed if she'd still been alive. "I've lived with it this far. I can continue living with the knowledge that some people are just selfish and don't care about anyone but themselves."

Chad tucked his head under my chin. "A lot of people are like that." His father, yes. Exactly like mine. But his father had had mates too, who might, or might not, have had a thing for Chad. He was convinced one of them had, but it could've just been his manic paranoia. So I wasn't sure what to believe.

All I knew was that he'd been broken and beaten on for most of his life—but it was over now.

I stroked his back with a sure hand, applying pressure to let him properly feel it. He sighed softly and relaxed against me.

Jeremy's hand was still splayed on my stomach, and he was eying the two of us with a look of... was that fondness? How could we possibly have got this far, that Jeremy watched me cuddle Chad with fondness? Had he before, without me noticing? Didn't it bother him even a little bit anymore?

Jeremy met my eyes and he smiled slightly. *"I love you,"* he mouthed.

I wondered for a moment why he didn't say it out loud, but then figured he might not feel that strongly for Chad just yet, and saying those words only to me would rub that in.

I loved them both. Falling for my own student was the most unethical thing I'd ever done, but I didn't regret it.

And he wasn't my student anymore.

Chad was mine—*our*—boyfriend now, and all the bad things in his life had been replaced with something good.

At least I hoped he saw it like that, because I sure did. The three of us, we were good together, no matter how we'd started.

"Can we sleep? I'm knackered." My eyes threatened to fall shut.

"Yeah. It's getting late, anyway." Jeremy bent over to kiss me, then the mattress moved as he got out of bed.

Chad pushed away from me too and I watched their backs disappear into the bathroom together.

I smiled to myself as I rolled over on my side. I

must've blacked out immediately, because I couldn't remember them getting back into bed, but when I woke up the next morning, I found them spooned together. Chad the little spoon and Jeremy the big one.

And that was when I knew, with certainty, that we'd be okay. That we'd make it work, this three way relationship of ours. That we'd be fine.

Because it wasn't just me and Jeremy, and me and Chad. It was Chad and Jeremy as well, and the sight of the two of them spooning like that made my heart swell.

CHAPTER 19

*C*had went to see both his psychiatrist and doctor the minute we stepped off the train at King's Cross. He'd got appointments with both after ringing them once he'd got up in the morning.

Jeremy and I headed to the Café to wait for him there, as he planned on going there afterwards anyway. We were hungry too, so the thought of food made us both hurry up.

Harriet was at the counter once we entered, and she glanced up as the bell rung, bowed her head to what she was doing, before her attention shot back to us. "Hey!" She came round the counter to meet us. "Where's Chad?"

"Doctor and psychiatrist appointments." I shook her hand. Chad's aunt was a good person, who cared a lot about her nephew, and who hadn't once voiced any sort of discomfort or disagreement or even curiosity about our relationship with Chad. She'd accepted us as easily as she accepted him, and *that* was the unconditional love close family should have for each other.

"Is he okay?" She glanced anxiously between us.

"His dosage is too low. He needs a higher one, or new medicine. I don't know. I trust the doctors to do what they feel will be best for him." They were the ones with the knowledge, after all.

Harriet chewed her bottom lip, like Chad tended to do when he was nervous. "What did he do?"

"Rapid cycled. But it's okay. We managed it." As well as was possible. If Chad had continued to be angry, we might not have, but he'd spiralled back down into depression, which was actually easier to deal with than irritability, anger, and paranoia.

Harriet let out a shaky breath. "How was the funeral?"

I didn't bother telling her I hadn't participated in it, because that would make her worry all the more, so I only said, "Like a regular funeral." Not that I'd ever been through an entire funeral before, but then again, I presumed they were all mostly the same.

Harriet nodded, then some of her usual bright

smile came back. "Do you want anything? It's on the house."

We ordered sandwiches, but I refused to get it for free, and paid for both Jeremy and I. Though, with Jeremy working there he apparently got a discount, and I grudgingly agreed to get the same discount when Harriet said she wouldn't take a pound more.

So we took a seat at a table, while Harriet stayed behind the counter to cheerfully greet customers who'd come in after us.

"You've been quiet today." I watched Jeremy closely from where I sat opposite him. "Are you all right?"

He blinked, surprised. "Yeah. I'm fine." He seemed thoughtful though, so I wasn't sure I believed him. "I just... like Chad said, it was awkward at first, you know? But now... I feel like we're finding our footing."

"Did you bond on your walk yesterday?" I hoped they had. I hoped they'd spoken together and got every single thing out in the open.

"Yeah, of course we did. About everything, but we've been over it all before too, so it wasn't anything *new*. But yeah, it's nice to spend time with him alone too." He smiled sheepishly. "I hope you don't mind, but, yeah, two-on-two time is good. I get to know him better when it's just the two of us."

"Spending time together is important, in couples and all three of us together." As long as we managed this without anyone getting jealous, it was a win. And I was happy they wanted to spend time together, because that meant that they were moving ahead. That they weren't just moving ahead with me, but staying in a stand-still with each other.

"I've also been thinking about my parents." Jeremy tipped his head back to stare up at the ceiling. "How am I going to even begin to explain our new situation? This new relationship, how it all fits together, the new living arrangements, sleeping arrangements—"

"I don't think your parents need to know about our sleeping arrangements," I cut in, horrified at the thought of explaining to Jeremy's mum, the sweetest lady I'd ever met, something like that.

"Well, she'll know we all share the same bed when she finds out she can still come for a visit, as we still have an available guest room."

"Isn't it better that we all share a bed? Doesn't that prove how serious it is? If one of us had kept the guest room, it might've seemed like... I don't know, like one of us weren't equal, like it was just for the sex." I glanced round uncomfortably once that came out, as we were in a public place with people around us. Thankfully, no one seemed to have heard me. Or no one made a show of looking at us if they'd heard.

Then again, we were in Soho, the gay part of London. Maybe people were more open down here, seeing as threesome sex was quite common in the gay community.

Or so I'd heard, it wasn't like I'd ever been a proper part of it. I was never out clubbing or pulling blokes.

Jeremy groaned and pressed the back of his hands to his eyes. "My parents are loving and committed, and they never minded me being gay or being with you. In fact, they love you too. But I don't think they'll be as understanding about a relationship between three people. They're old and it's... controversial and certainly not the norm "

"Don't worry so much." I knew exactly what Jeremy's parents were like, and I honestly didn't think he had anything to worry about. Yes, they might not understand, not at first, but they would never stop speaking to their son. "We'll cross that bridge once we get to it."

"Easy for you to say. It's not you she's ringing every week." Another groan. "I feel like I'm lying to her, you know? And I hate that. She's also asking when we're coming back up for a visit. It's not like we can just show up with Chad unannounced either."

That was true. "You can head up a day or a weekend you're not working and explain it to them."

"Yeah, I guess." Jeremy rubbed his chin thoughtfully.

Our sandwiches arrived, carried over by a smiling Harriet. "Is Chad stopping by once he's done with his appointments?"

"That's the plan." My stomach grumbled at the sight of the thick sandwich, filled up with roast beef, salad, and topping. "Though it might take a while."

"I'll be here for hours still." Harriet swept back to the counter, leaving me and Jeremy alone to enjoy our lunch.

"Do you realise that in ten days or so, it'll be two months since you met Chad?" I kept count. Who could blame me? In two months, we'd moved from separate bedrooms, to adding Chad into our relationship, to all three of us sharing a bed.

"Time sure flies." Jeremy took a big bite of his sandwich. His was a simpler ham and cheese, but he seemed to enjoy it equally as much as I enjoyed my beef. "It doesn't feel that long."

I'd known Chad for nine months now. I'd noticed him that first day of the term when he'd slouched into my class, though not in a sexual way back then.

I'd been worried about him, about his bruises, about him not participating at all, the few assignments he'd handed in riddled with spelling mistakes and wrong word-usage, and pretty much not understandable.

I'd tried to get him to test for dyslexia so many times, but he'd always refused. And then I'd gone and got attached to him, and slept with him—and then he'd quit.

We finished our sandwiches, and I'd emptied two cups of coffee while Jeremy had a cup of tea, when Chad finally came into the Café. He looked around, then his face broke into a brilliant smile that made my heart skip as he saw us.

"New medicine." He held up a bag as he sat down on a chair. "Well, same medicine and dosage on the antipsychotics, but new mood stabilisers. And they drew, like, half my blood, I swear." He patted the inside of his elbow gingerly, where he must have a piece of cotton taped over the skin where the needle had pierced.

Then he glanced towards the counter, where Harriet was busy with a customer. "I wonder who's working today. I should apologise—"

He hadn't even finished speaking when someone entered, causing the bell to ring. It drew his attention and he jumped up all of a sudden, blocking the path for two blokes—one blond, the other black-haired.

"Damian!" He gulped nervously. "I—I'm *so* sorry. I didn't mean to kick you. Not *there*." His eyes flickered down to the black-haired bloke's groin—and that was when I remembered. Chad had kicked him right in his package in his manic anger.

"That's okay." His—Damian's?—face was stony though, but I wasn't sure if that was because he was still mad or not. Being kicked in the nuts was no pleasant experience, but Chad had a mental illness *and* he was apologising for what he'd done, so I hoped he wouldn't continue to stay mad at him. He deserved another chance.

"Hey, Josh." Chad bowed his head to the blond bloke, blushing slightly. "I'm sorry if—" He motioned to Damian, who cast him a confused look.

Josh seemed to get the meaning though. "That's okay." He smiled softly. "I hope you're feeling better."

"I am. I will, anyway." He drew his bag further in against his side, weighing it, as if making sure it was really there.

"I've got to work," Damian said, and brushed past Chad without anything else.

"He's real mad, isn't he?" Chad asked Josh, who'd stayed put.

"Not really. He understands. He deals with me day in and day out, so—nothing can compare to that,

I think." Josh smiled softly again, then he followed Damian into the back room.

"That was Angelina's son Josh," Chad said when he sat back down again. "And his boyfriend. Whom I work with. Whom I kicked." The last explanation was for my benefit, as Jeremy must know who he was, considering he worked here too.

"Is Josh bipolar too?" I asked, as it'd sounded like they had something in common from his parting words.

"No. He's..." Chad chewed on his bottom lip. "What was it again? Borderline? Yes! He's borderline. It's a personality disorder."

"Chad!" Harriet had finished with the customers at the counter, and now she wrapped her arms tight around Chad's neck, almost choking him in her eagerness to give him a cuddle. "I'm so happy to see you. How was your appointments?"

He coughed a bit as she released her grip around him. "It was okay, I guess. New medicine."

"I hope this one's more suitable. Oh—I'll be back soon." Another customer stood at the counter, and she bustled off.

Chad stared after her.

"She's worried about you," I offered, since he seemed a bit stunned at the sudden cuddle attack. "She loves you a lot."

TT KOVE

"Well, she has to. I'm her nephew."

"She doesn't have to love you just because you're related. She loves you because she genuinely cares." I bent forward and took his hand in mine, squeezing it. "She wants to be a part of your life."

"But what if the new medicine doesn't work either? Does she really want to be a part of it, if my bipolar disorder can't be controlled by medicine? Do *you* want to be a part of my life if I can't be controlled?"

"Hey." Now Jeremy leaned forward to take his other hand, depositing the bag on the table. "It's not just medicine that helps. A positive attitude goes a long way too. Not to mention that it's proven that healthy lifestyle choices helps bipolar people manage their disorder."

"What healthy lifestyle choices? Eating?"

"Yeah. Regular schedules. Eat at the same time every day, sleep at the same time and the same length every night, exercise, hobbies. There's a lot that can help, and it doesn't have to be medicine either." Seemed Jeremy really *had* read all the stuff I'd printed out about bipolar. It pleased me, that he'd taken all the information to heart.

"They said something about that in hospital, and my psychiatrist mentioned it too. I wasn't really listening." He bowed his head, mouth pursed. "I

224

don't see how that can help though. Lots of people lead lives like that. People who aren't mentally ill."

"Regular schedules lessen the stress of everyday life. If something's happening at a set time, you don't have to stress about it."

"Well, they say I should avoid stress." He lifted his head now, thoughtful. "And exercise could be a good thing. I'm not exactly in fit shape."

That was true. He was too thin. He needed a steady, healthy diet as well as proper exercise to build up his muscles.

"How about we start going to the gym together?" I suggested. That would be nice, right? Or perhaps seeing each other all sweaty and bothered would cause problems in the nether regions.

Chad liked the idea though, as he nodded enthusiastically. "Yeah, that'd be nice."

It'd been a while since I'd been to the gym myself. I'd used to go regularly before he'd crashed into my life again. Jeremy probably even longer, as he was a bit more relaxed about it. He didn't take it all that seriously. But then he was young yet, he might when he started gaining weight. And being a chef, there was a possibility of that happening.

He seemed to read my thoughts too, because he grinned at me, his eyes twinkling with humour.

I smirked back. It'd been a long-standing joke

between us before everything had happened. After Chad had come into the picture... it had fallen off the wayside, along with the gym itself.

But we'd get back to normal routine pretty soon, I knew it. As long as Chad's medicines started to have effect, he'd be more stable, and then we'd find proper footing in our new relationship.

I looked forward to it.

CHAPTER 20

*C*had's medicine seemed to help, and for the next few days he was in a mellow mood. And we did find our footing—things weren't as awkward as they'd been before.

At least it seemed that way to me, about them.

They were a lot more comfortable around each other, chatting, joking, and cuddling and kissing.

All three of us had Saturday off, so we decided that was the first day we went to the gym together. I lifted more than both of them combined, but I'd been lifting for a long time. Chad was the worst, as all the exercise he'd had in the past was sex, and you didn't exactly build a lot of muscles by that.

Well, okay, one could, and Chad was bendy, so apparently he'd been practicing for something.

After dinner, we settled on the sofas to watch a film. I took the smaller sofa, stretching out, and let them have the bigger one. They were the ones who were on shakier ground, so some time to cuddle for them would be good.

The film was good, but it couldn't quite hold my interest as I kept glancing over to them. They were sitting close together, sharing a bowl of popcorn.

We'd still only had sex together that one time and it was over a week ago. I wasn't someone who craved a shag all the time—but we were new and so were the feelings, and I *wanted* to be that close to the both of them again.

Chad eventually clued in to the fact I was staring at them, and he must've seen the heat in my eyes, because he grinned wickedly.

Jeremy, on the other hand, was oblivious, eyes glued to the telly.

"I'm taking a shower." Chad jumped up, almost toppling the bowl of popcorn.

"What? Now?" Jeremy glanced from him to the television and back again. "But the film—"

"Not that interesting." He all but ran into the bathroom, the door slamming shut behind him.

Jeremy turned wide eyes on me. "Is he getting manic again?"

"Nope. He's getting horny." And so was I. My

dick already pressed against the front of my trousers, and Jeremy's eyes took it in slowly.

"*Oh*." And just like that, the fire was lit in him as well.

The telly was forgotten, and I sat up to shut it off. I heard the shower run now that the noise from the film was gone, and I grinned. "You know what he wants, right?"

Jeremy's focus flitted to the bathroom door, then landed back on me. He nodded once. "Are we ready for this?"

"I think we are." I stood and walked over to him, bending down to kiss him passionately. He lent back, arching up towards me, hands gripping my waist.

Bending over like this was decidedly awkward though, and bound to give me a crick in the neck, so I pulled back. "Bed?" I took both of Jeremy's hands in mine, prying them from my hips and instead pulling him up on his feet.

The shower was still going as we passed the bathroom, and I couldn't help but grin. He must be taking Jeremy's already voiced phobia to heart and cleaning out good.

I got out of my clothes the minute I crossed the threshold in the bedroom, and Jeremy wasn't far behind me, throwing his own clothes to the side as well. We moulded together, our half-hard cocks lining up as he kissed, our hips rocking together.

"How are we going to do this?" He asked it against my lips, his brushing mine as he spoke, our breaths mixing.

"However we want to." I knew what I wanted once Chad joined us.

I wanted his arse—and I wasn't ashamed to admit it either. I wanted to rim him long and good, give him the experience of a lifetime—an experience where *his* pleasure was in focus, which I wasn't sure he'd ever been treated to before.

Whenever he spoke about it, it seemed like all the sex he'd had had been for his partners' benefits, of them just having their way with him. That wouldn't do.

The shower turned off, which meant Chad would be with us soon.

I slid my hands down to Jeremy's arse, taking both cheeks in my palms and squeezing.

Jeremy made a sound low in his throat and bucked against me. He might not like being fucked in the arse, but he didn't mind me touching it—or even feeling him back there, as long as I didn't press inside.

We were both rock hard now, lined up and slick in-between our bodies.

Light footsteps alerted me to another presence, and then Chad stepped across the threshold too, wearing a towel wrapped around his waist.

"Towel?" I reached out. The towel had to go.

His cheeks flushed slightly, gaze dropping to in-between our bodies. He licked his lips—and it was like something erupted from that small movement. He liked what he saw, his cock tenting the front of the towel.

I tugged on it and it fell loose, falling to the floor in a pool, leaving Chad standing naked in front of us. He was both shorter and thinner than Jeremy and I, but a lot of that had to do with his previous diet and habits.

"Come here." Jeremy pulled Chad in close, as I'd been busy just taking him in.

I'd seen him naked several times, even shagged him without Jeremy present, but it was like I was seeing him all over again. This time he was with *us*, not just me, and the simple thought made a fire start burning low in my stomach.

We were hesitant at first, kissing each other, rubbing together, but then we moved onto the bed and things started to progress.

I was dying to get my hands and mouth on Chad's arse, and as he sat staring at me with lust in his eyes, I decided it was time.

I put my hand on his back, gently pushing him forward so he was on his hands and knees. Then I squeezed both his arsecheeks in my palms, as I'd done to Jeremy earlier, I let my thumb rub over his opening, and it clenched under my touch.

Chad's head was bowed. It wasn't like he could see what I was doing anyway, braced on hands and knees as he was. But Jeremy's gaze was on me, steady and curious. I grinned wickedly at him, then parted the cheeks and bent in, licking over the tight, clenching muscle.

After meeting Jeremy, rimming hadn't been on the agenda. He'd never enjoyed any action back there, and I was okay with that with him. But Chad... Chad got off on arseplay—and so did I, and it was wonderful.

When I thrust my tongue in, the muscles clenched around me. A long, drawn-out moan escaped Chad and he pushed further back against me so my tongue slipped further in.

"Oh *God*." Chad's upper body fell to the bed, his face burying in the sheets.

"Anyone given you a proper rim job before?" I asked, back to licking over his entrance.

He shook his head, bunching the sheets around his head as he did so.

"Want to get the lube?" I motioned my chin

towards the bedside drawer behind Jeremy, who quickly did as asked, handing the half-full bottle my way before sitting up straight again. One hand lazily stroked his cock, which was still hard and ready.

Chad must've seen it too, because he gripped onto Jeremy's thigh, shaking him to gain Jeremy's attention. "Come over here. I'll suck you."

Jeremy didn't need to be told twice. He scooted over in front of Chad, who lifted himself up again and instead draped himself over Jeremy's lap, worshipping his cock.

"Fuck yeah." I watched another moment as Chad swallowed Jeremy down, then I squeezed lube out onto my fingers and continued with my set task. I licked him some more, spearing my tongue inside, then took my fingers to help to loosen him up properly.

Chad moaned as my finger sank in deep, opening him up more than my tongue could've ever done, though having a tongue in the arse brought its own kind of pleasure.

Jeremy's eyes had closed now, soft moans escaping him as Chad worked his mouth over his cock. They looked beautiful together like that, giving and being given pleasure.

I focused back on my task, of loosening Chad up enough to take my cock. So he could take us both, which had initially been his suggestion, and a thought and fantasy that hadn't left my mind since.

One finger, two fingers, three fingers, four fingers sliding in. He was bucking back, riding them, forcing my fingers in deeper, all the way to the knuckle.

He's ready.

I rose up on my knees, took hold of the base of my cock, and rubbed it in-between his arse-cheeks before pressing against the tight ring of muscles.

Chad popped off Jeremy's cock to moan loudly as I sunk into him, his body frozen and rigid, until I stilled once I was buried all the way inside him. "Breathe, love." I rubbed up his spine, and it seemed to work, because his body gradually relaxed around me and his face was back down in Jeremy's lap, mouth enveloping hard cock and sucking vigorously.

He was tight inside, clamping around me, and I closed my eyes and took deep breaths to stop myself from coming right then and there. It hadn't been *that* long since we'd shagged in the bathroom, or since all three of us had wanked off in the living room, but this... this was so *tight*.

Chad moved against me, spurring me into action as I thrust back, then in again. I gripped his hips with slick, lubed hands, holding him steady as I started thrusting in earnest, control gained back and pleasure to be had.

I didn't know how long we kept it going like that, but it must've been a while, because sweat was dripping down my forehead by the time I pulled out.

Chad looked at me over his shoulder, hand wrapped around Jeremy's dick, stroking it slowly.

"I want you both," he whispered, voice thick with lust.

The softly spoken words made my blood boil, and Jeremy's eyes widen as he realised what exactly it was Chad wanted.

Chad didn't waste any time. He grabbed the lube I'd discarded on the bed earlier, poured a good amount over Jeremy's cock and more over his hole, then he straddled Jeremy's lap and sank down on him in one swift movement.

My breath caught.

Seeing Jeremy enveloped by Chad's arse… *damn.* It was one of the hottest sights I'd ever seen, but I needed more. Chad wanted more. And I'd never done it before, and I was curious how it would feel.

After drizzling more lube over myself, I scooted over to straddle Jeremy's thighs too, then put my cock in position against Chad's entrance—and I pushed in.

It was tighter than before, a *lot* tighter, and the sensation of the muscles clenching on the upside of my cock, and feelings Jeremy's cock against the underside was almost enough to make me blow my load.

Almost.

I managed to rein it in, but only barely. I held still for what must've been at least a minute, maybe two, and all I could hear from them were heavy breathing as well. Then I gripped Chad's hips again and started moving.

"Aaahhh-*oh*!" Chad's body tensed, his head dropped, then fell back as he groaned loudly.

Jeremy's hands brushed over mine, settling further down on Chad's hips, holding him still and close as he adjusted to having two cocks inside him. He'd been all nonchalant about it when it was all talk, but actually doing it must be quite a different thing.

I didn't even like one in my arse, so I couldn't even imagine how full, and how much he must hurt, right now.

Something equal to a sob escaped Chad's throat, his eyes squeezed shut tightly.

"Hey, love, relax. Breathe." I kissed his neck, scraping my stubbled cheek against his skin as I knew he got off on it.

His lips were parted and Jeremy leaned in to place a soft kiss at the corner of them. "Is it too much?" His voice was a bit strangled too, at the completely new sensations we were experiencing pressed together inside Chad's body.

"N-no. Just a sec." Chad's head lolled back on my shoulders, his eyes blinking open slowly. "Oh God. This is so *good*."

I wasn't quite sure I believed that, as he clearly had a hard time adjusting.

He drew my head down for a kiss, then leaned in to kiss Jeremy. "You can move now," he said once he pulled back from the kiss, his arms wrapping around Jeremy's shoulders to hold himself steady.

I did; slowly at first, in case he was still in pain. But all I could hear from him was moans that grew in intensity as I quickened my speed.

Jeremy stayed calm, not moving at all, but he moaned too, so he must be getting enough pleasure from my cock sliding against his.

I sure felt like it was *too much* pleasure, and so did my balls as they pulled up, more than ready to shoot my load.

Not yet.

I needed this moment to continue. To be so intimately connected with the both of them for just a little bit longer.

I buried my face against Chad's neck, arms going around Chad's body to fumble for Jeremy. Once I found him, I pulled him in so close his chest pressed to Chad's, and then I locked my arms tight, holding us as close together as we could possibly come, all the while moving my pelvis, thrusting my cock in and out of Chad's body, up and against Jeremy's cock.

"Oh, fuck." It came out on a groan and Jeremy stiffened as he came, his come spurting inside Chad and over my cock, then slowly trickling down, making a mess of both of our balls.

Next Chad convulsed, crying out as he shot over Jeremy's stomach and chest. And bloody hell, but I managed to keep in control longer than the both of them! But once Chad's body started convulsing around me, I felt it coming, and I thrust in deep as I came, snapping my hips a couple of times to milk myself dry.

Jeremy lay down on his back, and Chad followed, draping over his body.

I pulled my softening cock out slowly, watched as Jeremy's softening one slipped out as well, then I collapsed to their side, boneless, listless, and completely sated. I could only flop my hand to the side, resting it atop the lower part of Chad's back, but it was enough to feel his skin—and Jeremy's too, against my forearm.

Our breathing was heavy in the otherwise quiet room, and the smell of sex was still heady. I gathered the rest of my strength and rolled over, plastering myself to their sides.

"I love you both so much," I whispered, nuzzling first Jeremy's neck, then Chad's. "So fucking much." I didn't think it was possible, before, to love two people like this, but I *did*.

They didn't answer, just smiled softly, and that was okay. I knew they loved me—but that they might not have got that far with each other yet. They liked each other, *adored* each other, but the whirlwind two months of all the drama wasn't enough to spark the love just yet.

But I knew they'd get there. I knew we'd be okay. Because what we had, it was special.

We'd worked for it, hurt for it, and been hurt for it, but we'd got here. The three of us in bed together, after having had one of the most intense sex of my life.

I didn't believe it would be smooth-sailing from here on out, because I knew it wouldn't be, but I simply knew we'd make it anyway.

Because we wanted it. We wanted *this*.

We wanted each other.

ABOUT THE AUTHOR

TT lives in Norway and writes about gay men living in Norway. She also occasionally writes about gay men living in the UK, because she loves the UK. Norway might be too cold for her, but TT doesn't like the summer, so she's learned to adapt. TT is happiest in front of her computer, creating emotional stories about men loving other men.

www.ttkove.com
ttkove@gmail.com

www.ingramcontent.com/pod-product-compliance
Lightning Source LLC
Chambersburg PA
CBHW031721170626
46808CB00005B/1842